I0658159

Sosa Gang 3

Romell Tukes

Lock Down Publications and Ca$h
Presents
Sosa Gang 3
A Novel by *Romell Tukes*

Romell Tukes

Lock Down Publications
Po Box 944
Stockbridge, Ga 30281

Visit our website @
www.lockdownpublications.com

Copyright 2023 by Romell Tukes
Sosa Gang 3

All rights reserved. No part of this book may be reproduced in any form or by electronic or mechanical means, including information storage and retrieval systems without permission in writing from the publisher, except by a reviewer who may quote brief passages in review.
First Edition April 2023
Printed in the United States of America

This is a work of fiction. Names, characters, places, and incidents either are products of the author's imagination or are used fictitiously. Any similarity to actual events or locales or persons, living or dead, is entirely coincidental.

Lock Down Publications
Like our page on Facebook: Lock Down Publications @
www.facebook.com/lockdownpublications.ldp
Book interior design by: **Shawn Walker**
Edited by: **Sunny Giovanni**

Stay Connected with Us!

Text **LOCKDOWN** to 22828 to stay up-to-date with new releases, sneak peaks, contests and more…
Thank you.

Submission Guideline.

Submit the first three chapters of your completed manuscript to ldpsubmissions@gmail.com, subject line: Your book's title. The manuscript must be in a .doc file and sent as an attachment. Document should be in Times New Roman, double spaced and in size 12 font. Also, provide your synopsis and full contact information. If sending multiple submissions, they must each be in a separate email.

Have a story but no way to send it electronically? You can still submit to LDP/Ca$h Presents. Send in the first three chapters, written or typed, of your completed manuscript to:

LDP: Submissions Dept
Po Box 944
Stockbridge, Ga 30281

DO NOT send original manuscript. Must be a duplicate.

Provide your synopsis and a cover letter containing your full contact information.

Thanks for considering LDP and Ca$h Presents.

Sosa Gang 3

Acknowledgements

First and foremost all praises are due to the most high Allah for guiding me through the ups and down to get me where I'm at today as a red man. Shout and much love to all the readers who fuck with me and support the kid. SHout the hometown YOnkers, NY (the whole 914), CB, YB, Lingo, SG, Baby James, Bonger, Brisco, the Cartels, Chino, and everybody fucking with Bama. Shout to my Bronx niggas, my Brooklyn team OG Chuck, GunnyTails, Lil YB and Curt from Brownsville, and Tim Dog. Shout to Philly OG Muchie, Big C, Dame, and Legs. Shout to Caliy, Texas, Miami, AH, Chi Raq, and coast to coast … Big Shout to LDP and ca$h for all there hard work and devotion in the game. Life is what you make it shoot for the stars and never less. Free everybody locked up in the state and fed free da real. Thanks to everybody support my vision, every book I make you will relate to it and feel that shit. There is only two endings in the street life if a person don't get out, so save yourself and your families the pain and hurt.

Romell Tukes

PROLOGUE
DOWNTOWN PHILLY

The courthouse was packed at noon today and Janasia wanted nothing but to enjoy her lunch break as she walked through the crowd of people to exit the courthouse. She'd been flooded with new cases, but one really caught her attention. A kid named Gee who was found in the back of a home in the suburbs.

Walking outside with her briefcase she wondered where she wanted to go eat. As Janasia approached her car, she saw a rose and a note on the windshield; a classic attention snatcher. Janasia couldn't help but smile, picking up the small note that read, *"12PM, Fogo De Choo, beautiful, Lex ..."*

Staring into the sky she realized how much of a gentleman he was, so she hopped in her car and went to the Fogo De Choo restaurant nearby for the lunch date as all types of thoughts filled up in her head.

When arriving at the restaurant, she saw Lez waiting out front on his phone. At first, she wondered who he was talking to. Her purse had her work pistol inside so if he tried anything, she would fry his ass in public.

"I thought you ain't talk to police." She approached him smiling, seeing him hang up his iPhone.

"You're DEA, not a cop. Your words." He joked.

"Whatever. But thank you for the rose. It was nice. I really need that."

"You're a queen. You shouldn't get nothing less. But let's have lunch," Lez told her, opening the door for her.

Janasia always felt chills when she got around him. Once seated, they chopped it up, then Janasia had something she felt was bothering her. "Can I trust you, Lez?"

"Trust me? Yes, but let me tell you dis. I will never fold, turn state, or violate my honor."

"Is that a yes or no?" She ain't wanna hear all that street talk. She heard it too many times until niggas started hearing double digit numbers.

"Yes."

"A man named Gee was recently murdered, and a snitch is trying to frame your ex, Foxy."

"How do you know that, ma?"

"I know a lot of things. But anyways, it's a lot of snake shit going on with the Outlaws, and soon the person trying to frame her will be trying to take you down. So, I just wanted to give you a heads up," she told him.

"Who is the person?"

"The crazy shit is, it's her own father, Kane, trying to frame her on the body. He turned in a truck and wiretaps because Gee started working with the Feds. That's another thing. The Feds are in town and a woman is trying to nail some big boys."

"I heard," Lez said.

"So, why are you still in the streets? Look, I want to help you. Lez, I don't want to see you go down, so I've been trying to save you and your crew, but this is getting tense."

"I know, and I thank you for everything, Janasia, but I have to go."

"We ain't even get—"

"I'm sorry. I gotta go handle something." Lez stood up and leaned in, kissing her on the lips, and she didn't resist.

"Uhmmmmm," she moaned, opening her eyes to see he was gone. That kiss touched her soul. She never felt something so special. Janasia hoped Lez would be smarter than the rest of his gang.

Janasia felt by telling him the info he would fall back and take himself away from the bullshit going on. Her pussy was so creamy she started to imagine what his dick game was like if that one kiss had her gushy.

***

PHILADELPHIA INTERNATIONAL AIRPORT
HOURS LATER

Lez had to reach out to Foxy on her Facebook and tell her it was important, and he needed to meet her ASAP. Foxy gave him the airport's location. Lez felt like if he told Foxy about her dad then maybe she would show down. Lez ain't wish jail on his worst enemy, and deep down he still cared for Foxy.

A Benz coupe pulled through the car lot, speeding as he saw a plane take off.

Foxy hopped out with a Draco in her hand, but Lez stood in front of his car knowing she would've been shot if she wanted him dead. "I should kill you right now, nigga," Foxy said.

"Foxy, I called to save your life."

"Save me?" She laughed then got serious.

"Look, the Feds are on you and Kane is working for them, trying to take you down. He ratted on Wayne, too. That's how he got out of jail."

"Nigga, I should blow your fuckin' brains out for disrespecting me and my pops." She was mad.

"He telling on how you killed Gee. We got the truck you used. He's working with Feds. A DEA lady told me."

Foxy knew there had to be some truth to it because her dad was the only person who knew she killed Gee and used a truck to slide in. Kane also told her where to hide the truck and she gave Kane the murder weapon so he could get rid of it, but he was thirsty for the gun. Foxy started thinking back to other events that made her think Kane was moving snakey. "Fuck!" she shouted.

"Be smart. Foxy, he's dangerous. Save yourself," Lez told her.

"This shit is all because of ya'll niggas," she yelled.

"I ain't know you was in this shit, Foxy, and on the opposite. Come on, we go way back," Lex said as a Lexus creeped up from behind them and opened fired on them both.

Tat…Tat…Tat…Tat…

Foxy got hit twice and Lez once in his shoulder before shooting back and trying to save Foxy at the same time. When he saw Sosa firing, he almost dropped his gun as bullets continued to fly.

Tat… Tat… Tat… Tat… Tat… Tat… Tat… Tat…

The Lexus raced off as the airport cops came from the Gate 4 area, rushing to the gun fire. Lez took Foxy's Draco, tossing it in his car. She was still breathing as he helped save her life until EMT came.

***

SOUTH PHILLY

Sosa drove into 5th Street Projects to pick up Lil Jet, who was awaiting him so they can go on their mission, but Sosa couldn't believe what he just witnessed.

Allure needed a ride to the airport and Sosa took her so she could catch her flight to Atlanta for a photoshoot. Before he left the airport, he couldn't believe his eyes when he saw Lez talking to Foxy on some snake shit.

Sosa felt betrayal from his friend so he decided to make a move that would change everything with them. He knew about Lez and Foxy's relationship in the past, but shit was real in the streets right now. He ain't know who to trust.

If Sosa had to doubt one of his man's loyalty or trust, then he didn't need them around him. Making choice to shoot at both of them is something he was willing to live with and deal with whatever comes after.

Lil Jet was on the block with a few killers when Sosa pulled up, rolling down his window.

"You ready?" Sosa asked Lil Jet, who hopped off of the stairs.

"Yeah." Lil Jet shared some words with his young bulls, who were block huggers.

"Shit about to go sideways soon," Sosa told him when he pulled off onto the dark, scary Philly streets.

"What you mean?"

"I saw Lez and Foxy meeting up at the airport on some sneaking shit, so I sent shots at both of them a few minutes ago." Sosa made a left at the end of the block, seeing police harass niggas on his right.

"What?" Lil Jet couldn't believe it.

"Yeah bro, I think we was about to cross us, so I made the first move, bull. I ain't finna let him fuck us over," Sosa explained.

"He dead?"

"Nah, so we need to be a step ahead," Sosa stated.

"I think you should have at least asked Lez what happened before sliding on the bro. He still Sosa Gang." Lil Jet made sense and Sosa felt the same way.

"I know but it looked too shady and I ain't want to take no chances," Sosa says, feeling a little bad for not thinking shit out.

"That was a bad call but I'm with you. There is no turning back now, cuz."

"I know," Sosa added, driving towards uptown.

***

CLUB ACES, PHILLY

Wayne and a few of his boys were in the club having a ball. They were buying up all the expensive liquor and fucking with the baddest bitches in the club.

Tonight, was Wayne's birthday and he just wanted to drink and wash his pain away with the liquor.

Roddy's funeral was a mess. Never could he imagine someone really shooting up a church on some mad man, movie type shit.

Wayne hadn't been the same since Roddy's death. He didn't care about life itself no more. He ain't even want to sell drugs no more. The only thing on Wayne's mind was kill.

While in prison, he told himself that he would never go back to feeling like this and now he was back at square one.

"I'ma be back," Wayne told everybody.

"Where you going?" A sexy, thick, dark skinned chick with green eye contacts asked, trying to leave with Wayne tonight.

"To take a fucking piss. I'll be back in a second." Wayne walked out of the booth. He was a little tipsy making his way through the crowds of people.

Wayne hated being in tight spaces like clubs, especially dark spots. He had been in and out of jail his whole life, so he still had a prison mindset.

Luckily, the mens bathroom was empty. He rushed inside to take a urine because the liquor was running through his liver.

As he took a piss, he didn't see the two men dressed in black hoodies inside of a club, sneak inside.

A swing to his back made him jump back but that didn't stop the blows. Both had knives in their hands as they attacked Wayne, stabbing him in his neck, chest, heart, and organs repeatedly.

A dude walked into the restroom, seeing what was taking place and left scared to death.

Wayne's body was tossed in the toilet stall after he was stabbed over eighty two times.

Sosa and Lil Jet walked out of the club like it was nothing, exiting with their hoodies on.

Outside, they got in the car but as they were about to pull off, five D.C. Crew niggas saw them get in the car and opened fire on them.

The person who ran with them went to tell them two dudes were in the restroom stabbing Wayne up.

"Oh shit." Lil Jet ducked the bullets closing the car door as Sosa burned rubber, getting the fuck from out of there.

Sosa thought it would be good and quiet to bring knives in the club, so they didn't have to make too much noise. The gang made an agreement to kill Wayne because he was all for himself and his crew. To only make shit worse, the Feds wanted him and the gang ain't need that attention.

"You think them niggas knew it was us?" Lil Jet asked.

"Fuck it, if they do," Sosa stated knowing more problems were about to follow up after Wayne's death.

***

NICETOWN, PHILLY
ONE MONTH LATER

OG Kane, Foxy and Rizzy all attended the meeting in a building Kane rented out for the day.

"Today is a big day because as you know, there is two more Outlaw leading members that the both of you never met but today you will. We lost Gee and Max and that's a part of the game.

14

I ain't lose no sleep but it's time we elevate," Kane said.

"What happen to Sosa Gang?" Rizzy asked.

"Fuck 'em. They can't stop us, Rizzy. We locking the streets down and our crew is growing every day. Special thanks to my lovely daughter and you." Kane saw Foxy fake smile.

"Before I bring out the two leaders, I have a special guest," Kane said as he yelled for two men to bring out the surprise.

There was a wheelchair and a man with black pillowcase over his head was seated in it. The two men left the wheelchair there and walked off.

"Who dat?" Foxy asked.

"One less problem," Kane got up and snatched the pillowcase off the man's head.

Twin's face was bloody with duct tape covering his mouth. Kane caught Twin slipping two nights ago and had his goon kidnap him.

"Ain't this some shit?" Rizzy clutched his weapon.

"I'ma bringing out our guests. First person, come out," Kane said as Foxy and Rizzy broke their necks to see who else had a seat at the table.

Janasia walked out in a suit and the look on Foxy's face said it all. She knew who the woman was.

"She DEA," Foxy said

"Yes, but she is also a leading member for over ten years. Her father basically started the Outlaws with the help of the next man, who is also my plug," Kane said as his next guest walked out.

A tall man with a Muslim beard came out wearing a garment and giving Janasia a hug. He hadn't seen her in years because they both played the background. They let the other members run the show, but it was time they stepped in.

When Twin saw the man with the beard, he couldn't believe it as he had been listening to every word.

Twin's heart almost dropped as he looked at his father, Imam Ahmad.

"They had been running the show from behind the scenes for years, especially Ahmad.

"It's nice to meet y'all, Foxy and Rizzy, but starting today new rules will be placed and things will change," Imam Ahmad said, seeing an awkward look on all of their faces.

"This is very past due," Janasia said as her and Imam Ahmad pulled out guns.

Boc... Boc... Boc... Boc... Boc... Boc... Boc... Boc...

They aired Kane's body out with bullets before two men ran in the room to remove Kane's dead body. Foxy and Rizzy couldn't believe what just went down so fast.

"Do you have a problem with us killing your rat ass father?" Janasia asked Foxy as she saw her look as if Foxy wanted to try something.

"Not at all," Foxy replied.

"Good. Now, let's get down to business and get to a bag," Janasia said.

"First off, let me start by saying this is my son right here," Imam Ahmad said cutting off Twin's wrist and ankle tapes. Then, removing his tape on his face.

Foxy and Rizzy couldn't adjust to everything they had been seeing in the last five minutes.

"Dad, what the fuck is going on?" Twin stood up.

"I'ma give you an option to either take Kane's position in the Outlaws or you can die with your friend. Twin, you have seventy-two hours to make your choice," Imam Ahmad said before four men escorted Twin out the building and letting him go free.

"I don't think that was smart to let him go," Rizzy said

"Did I ask you?" Imam Ahmad looked at Rizzy, who shut up.

"This is a new quarter, and we got some shit planned. We just have to clean up some loose ends," Janasia said ice grilling Foxy and peeping her dirty looks.

"There will be more bodies, more money, and more drama now. Be ready. We all family now, Janasia and Foxy," Imam Ahmad said before turning to leave.

Rizzy knew shit was about to get real spicy.

Foxy got up and left, thinking about how they just murked Kane right in front of her. She wanted to kill him herself, so she wasn't feeling how they did that in front of her. Janasia walked out laughing with Rizzy behind her, ready for this new chapter.

***

PHILLY, PA

Sosa ordered a private jet to take him to Miami so he could get away and spend some time alone at his condo that he copped. Shit was getting odd. Everybody had been acting funny. Twin became nowhere to be found and Lez became a ghost. He just needed to clear his thoughts and reconnect with his inner self. Sosa took a nap on the private jet. This was the first nap he took in almost two days.

***

Hours later, Sosa woke up realizing he had been asleep close to five hours and the jet was just landing. He knew it only took two hours the most to get to Miami on a plane and a jet was much faster.

Looking out the window Sosa saw all types of tropical trees and a different environment. Sosa knew he wasn't in Miami at all, especially when he saw six trucks pull up and surround the jet.

Sosa grabbed his gun and went to the pilot cabin, but the door was locked and bulletproof.

"Fuck." Sosa knew it was a setup, so he figured why not go out with a bang. He opened the door and saw over twenty Spanish looking men waiting on him.

When he was about to start busting his Glock 22 with a thirty-two-shot clip, he saw a pretty older woman get out of one of the trucks in a black dress. The closer she got, he was shocked to see it was his mom.

"We have to go, son. Welcome to Colombia. Come give mommy a hug," Sosa's mom said, smiling as he got off the jet confused ...

Romell Tukes

CHAPTER 1
MEDELLIN, COLOMBIA

Sosa climbed in one of the SUV's with his mom, never seeing her so alive and even able to talk. He didn't know what the fuck was really going on, seeing a bunch of Colombians all over the place, waiting for Ashley to get in the truck.

Ashley got inside the truck and stared at her son, telling the driver to go. "I know this may look weird or strange, even though it is, but there is a lot you don't know about me and your bitch ass father," she said, crossing her leg, looking into the beautiful city of Medellin.

"I thought you was fucked up," Sosa said, thinking his mom had mental problems. The last time he went to see her in Atlanta at a mental house, Ashley was zoned out and fucked up off meds the people there were given her.

"That was an out, baby. The Feds been on me for a long time, and the only way to succeed in the world is to think ahead, so I did while still running a drug enterprise. I know your dad told you a lot of stories of why I left, but I'ma tell you the truth, now. I've been waiting on this day," Ashley said as they got closer to her home in the hills she had for years.

"I heard some many stories. I honestly don't know what to believe."

"While I'll never lie to you, son, you're here for a reason, today, son; trust me," she told him, looking at how handsome he was.

"Why the fuck am I here anyway?" Sosa asked as the SUV drove up a big hill.

"How about you chill out and watch your fucking mouth when you talk to me? I'm still your mother." She gave him an evil eye.

"Sorry." Sosa saw the trucks pull up into a long driveway filled in with bricks and stone to match the European French-style mansion.

Ashley got out the truck and Sosa followed her, looking at guards armed with weapons, dressed in camouflage. Sosa thought he was in a dream. There was no way his mom had been living like this. It didn't add up.

The double doors opened, and the white marble floors and high ceilings stood out. There was an antique design mural on the walls.

"Damn." He followed her into the living room.

"You like it?" she asked, sitting down.

"It's cool." Sosa looked at the stone fireplace in the spacious living room that was the size of a club.

"When you were born, then Zarhya, I thought life couldn't have been no better for me and my family," she said looking at photos she had of all her kids years ago.

"So, what happened?" Sosa wanted the truth since he was a kid because he felt like his life wasn't complete until he knew why his mom left and understood her reason.

"Your father started cheating on me which was cool. I ain't care. But when he snitched on my brother, that was my breaking point. I moved. I tried to take y'all, but he threatened me with a murder he saw me do when we first met. When I left, I got married to my brother's plug out here and laid low for some years and started opening shop in the States with my husband until he got killed," Ashley said sadly as she pulled a cigarette out her purse and blew the smoke into the air.

"They killed your husband for what?" Sosa asked.

"Who are they?"

"I figured a cartel family or something living out here," Sosa stated.

"Nah, I killed him, Sean, and my life changed. I went crazy for a while over his death. It was the worst point in my life."

"But you killed him?"

"You ever killed someone you loved?" Ashley asked, looking at him.

"Maybe. I don't know," Sosa replied, trying to see where she was going with this.

"So, you ain't love your brother?" Ashley gave him a wicked smile.

"You know about that?"

"I know a lot, Sean, and killing Block was good, but Barry knew you would play right into his hand," she said as a maid came out with glasses of liquor on a tray.

"How did you know that if you were in a hospital?"

"I sneaked out at night for a long time. I knew about your crew. The way you handle the beef was smart, but your new beef is gonna be amongst some serious people."

"I know, mom, and I'ma be ready."

"Let's hope so, but your downfall will be Barry and Vero."

"Vero?"

"Oh, you don't know your little girlfriend's mom is the sister of my number one enemy— the Cubans? We have been having drugs wars for years, and now I took over my husband's bussy, they will do anything to kill me and you."

"Me?" Sosa asked,

"They know who the fuck you are, Sosa; trust me," she said.

Sosa couldn't believe what he was hearing, but he knew deep down his mom would not lie to him. "I need a plug?" Sosa asked

"I know, son. That's why you're here, because I need a favor, too," she said getting, down to the business of why he was really there.

"What's that?"

"This may sound crazy, but I need you to kill Barry. The Feds are about to crash down on him and he's gonna tell on everybody; even your black ass; so, this is gonna take some balls that I know you have, son. I seen your work and I was a little surprised."

"What for? I got your blood in me. I heard how you used to do."

"I'm a changed woman. I became a thinker and learned to conduct business off impulse and not emotion because emotion will get you killed."

"That's why you want me to kill Barry instead of you?" Sosa asked.

"You're very smart, Sean. It still hurts me that I was not around to raise all of you, especially Zarhya."

"She needed you the most," Sosa added.

"I know. One day, I'ma be able to sit down with her and tell my story."

"Zarhya is hard at forgiving, Mom. With her, it'll take time. A lot. Trust me. She is still resentful and heartbroken, but Barry did a good job at raising us whether you like him or not." Sosa spoke the truth and she had no choice but to respect it.

"That's good, but it's clear Block didn't get the same type of love. But, on another note, you need to check your inner crew," she said, taking a sip of her drink.

"My crew loyal to me."

"You're sure about that, Sosa?" Ashley got up and walked off, coming back with a photo book.

"Yeah, they never showed me any signs of disloyalty or a reason to mistrust them." Sosa stuck up for his gang.

"The guy dressed up in an Islamic garment, do you know who he is?" She handed him the photo book she kept in the cut for years."

"Yeah, that's my friend's dad, Imam Ahmad." Sosa had a crazy look on his face.

"He runs the Outlaws with this woman also." Ashley handed him a pic of Janasia.

"That's the DEA bitch. Oh, shit."

"She is a dangerous woman and smart, son, so be careful, okay?"

Sosa couldn't believe he missed all of this, but now he wondered if Twin was lining him up all along. The feeling of having to second guess someone so close was hard because without any form of trust in the business, shit would crumble before his eyes.

"This is a lot, right here. I'ma need to figure it out." Sosa's head felt like it was spinning.

"Word of advice?"

"Your advice as a mom, a killer, or a businesswoman?"

"A mom right now. Never put your trust in a man or woman. Especially me," Ashley said, standing up to leave him in his thoughts.

CHAPTER 2
CHESTNUT HILL, PA
ONE MONTH LATER

Twin had been hiding out at his new crib in the suburbs, thinking about his next move in life because it could be his last. When the Outlaws kidnapped him, he knew they would fo'sho kill him and leave his ass stanking in a ditch somewhere. At their meeting, Twin heard everything and he couldn't believe what took place. To see his dad being one of the Outlaw leaders was some shit he would never expect. Imam Ahmad gave him a choice to be down with the Outlaws or die, and that was last month where he had 72 hours to make a decision but he had been hiding out since.

Sosa changed his number, Lil Hak was holding down the gang. Lil Jet was taking care of his seed with Beth, trying to lay low. When everybody heard about the Feds, niggas got spooked and got ghost. Lez hadn't been in touch with Twin in a while, but he heard what happened, so shit was about to be crazy.

Twin had been spending time thinking which side he was about to choose because the gang were his friends, and his dad is family. Crossing sided would be some sucker shit in Twin's head, but the situation wasn't a regular one, especially when love would be lost from it.

A noise awoke Twin from his nap. He jumped out of bed and grabbed his AR assault rifle, creeping towards the kitchen where he heard the noise from. Twin walked barefooted on the cherry wood floor, hoping whoever was in there didn't hear him so he could blow a hole in their face.

Entering the kitchen, he saw a familiar face sitting on a stool with a gun on the countertop. "Sosa?"

"Twin. Good to see you, young bull. Nice pad here. You been stacking bread," Sosa said, looking at Twin's dangled AR.

"What the fuck are you doing here?" Twin took a seat on the other side of the counter.

"We need to talk, because from the looks of shit, our gang is about be divided into sets. Some may even be with the enemy." Sosa gave him a stern, uncomfortable look.

"I got kidnapped by the Outlaws last month, and you are not gonna believe what I saw," Twin said, putting the assault rifle down.

"Man, I'll believe anything nowadays."

"My dad is one of the leaders, and that DEA bitch."

"Damn," says Sosa, nonchalantly.

"You knew?"

"Somewhat, but this is bigger than we both could ever imagine."

"What the fuck you mean?"

"I'ma get to that, but I need to know where we stand, because if your dad runs them and you're alive, my mind can only put a few things together," Sosa said, staring Twin in his eyes like a man as his dad taught him.

"You questioning my loyalty?" Twin looked like he got offended.

"Hell yeah, bro. Shit getting real. Lez turned on us and I don't know who next, so I need to know where we stand— enemies or friends?" Sosa's hand was close to his gun just in case Twin got crazy. Sosa already had his mind made up, and if niggas weren't with him, then they were against him which meant war time.

"That's my dad, bro, and you my best friend," Twin said

"I understand that, but you have to choose a side, bro, because things are about to get nasty. I'ma be real, bull. I'm not sparing a soul because they not the Outlaws or D.C. Crew."

"I picked a side already, and I'ma stay on my side. I love ya'll niggas. If I gotta go against my dad, then so be it." Twin's words were like music to his ears.

"You had my heart racing for a second." Sosa took a deep breath.

"If I would've said my dad, what would have you done?" Twin asked, seeing his boy inch towards his gun the whole conversation.

"Smoked your ass, nigga. What the fuck? You think I would've let myself walk out of here knowing a killer like yourself would hop on my line?"

"Smart nigga." Twin laughed

"I went to Miami to get away, and someone hijacked the plane and took me to Colombia."

"Damn. What happened in Colombia?"

"My mom lived out there and was there with a gang of niggas. I couldn't believe that shit, bro. You had to be there to see that shit, my nigga. No lie." Sosa said.

"What happened with your mom, bro? I thought she was in a mental hospital or some shit?" Twin remembers talking to Sosa about his mom, daily.

"I thought she was, but this bitch a plug," Sosa told him. "Yeah, I was fucked up about it when I first heard, bull."

"Damn. What she say, because we gonna need a new plug soon, right?"

"I gotta do her a solid and she got us, bro."

"You think she trustworthy, bro? I mean, I know she your mom, but my dad just tried to kill me, so I wouldn't put too much trust into her," Twin said, still fucked up about his dad giving him a choice to be a part of his crew or die.

"Sometimes, in certain situations, you have to give a person trust until they show you otherwise." Sosa knew his mom wanted his dad dead and that was a fair exchange to him.

"What we gonna do about the Outlaws? They killed Kane."

"They killed Kane?" Sosa couldn't believe it, but it didn't make sense.

"He was a rat this whole time, bro. I guess what Wayne was pushing about him is valid and true because my dad and Janasia smoked that nigga right in front of my face." Twin remembered the brutal scene.

"I can't believe Janasia a cold-blooded bitch like that. She was really into Lez," Sosa said.

"Well, Foxy and her both gonna have a hard time getting along."

"Fuck that nigga."

"It's on sight with him now, cuz, just know that," Sosa said.

"I'm already sharp, bro. Facts. I'm with you, but we got another problem besides the Outlaws," Twin said.

"What now, bull? We got enough of shit on our plate."

"What about that Wayne shit? I bet niggas looking for us."

"How you hear 'bout that because I know you been hiding out in here? Nobody saw you?" Sosa said. He went through to find Twin.

"I saw it on social media. These dumb niggas out here posting up everything."

"Who?"

"Dirty T."

"I heard of him. He Wayne cousin or some shit who lived in Chester?" Sosa asked, hearing Wayne talk about him before.

"Yeah. That the bull he a wild boy, too, so we gotta lay him down."

"Agreed," Sosa added.

"Lil Hak out there holdin' shit down by himself, bro." Twin felt like Lil Hak was in the field keeping them alive.

"I know, but now he got cuz. It's no need for hiding, bro. This shit already started, my nigga. Get for a war." Sosa hugged his friend and left.

CHAPTER 3
SOUTHWEST PHILLY

Lil Hak woke up next to his gun and a sexy brown skin chick he met last night in a club. "Ayo." He pushed the chick waking her up.

"Hmmmm?" She moved, still asleep.

"You ready?"

"For me to suck your dick?" she asked, fresh off a wake up, ready to put in work

"Hell nah. You bit my shit last night, little bitch."

"Oh, I'm sorry, daddy," she pled, hoping he was still about to trick on her because she knew he had that sack.

"It's cool, but you still gotta roll up out of here." Lil Hak got out of bed.

"I thought you said we gonna spend the whole day together?" She asked, sitting up now.

"That was before I fucked you." Lil Hak laughed, getting out the bed to help the young lady with her clothes.

"I'll get my own shit," she said upset, feeling played.

"Help yourself, then. I'm just trying to be a real gentleman."

"Whatever, dickhead." She got all her shit, rushing to get dressed.

"You know where the door at," he told her before walking to the shower in his apartment. Lil Hak got in the shower, hearing his front door slam hard. Today he had to go check on a few blocks on the west side which used to belong to Lez, but he jumped ship.

Hearing Lez out of all people cross sides did not feel right, but this was the game, and people changed every day, especially for the love of money or pussy.

Everybody been out of sight for the last month. Lil Hak ain't know what the fuck was going on, but something deep down told him some shit was about to pop off.

He turned on the hot water and just stood under it to clear his thoughts for a second. Life been moving so fast he felt like it was a dream instead of the real thing, but seeing his niggas die and go to jail made him see the reality of this street shit, day and night.

27

Sosa Gang had the streets but the Outlaws were still out here, and the D.C. Crew was run by a nigga name Dirty. Soon Lil Hak would need more work because he was getting low, but his boy became a ghost. Everybody knew about the DEA and FBI on their tail, so he figured Sosa was hiding out. Twin had to be doing the same thing because he disappeared also. There was some weird shit going on and he hoped everybody was okay, but he disliked the feeling of being left out.

Lil Hak turned off the hot water and grabbed the towel off the rack before looking at himself in the simi-fogged mirror. "I gotta get back in the gym," he told himself, seeing a gut appear. Walking back into his bedroom connected to his bathroom, he paused.

"You bitch, I'm not gonna let you play me," the woman who he just kicked out said with tears, pointing Lil Hak's 9-millimeter he kept on top of his dresser.

"Slow down, cutie. We aint gotta do this." Lil Hak tried to talk her down, but from the look on her face she wasn't going or falling for his word play.

"You just tried to play me," she shouted, looking like a mad woman.

"I'm sorry. You don't wanna do this. Trust me. Put the shit down."

"Fuck no. You got money on your head and I'ma collect it," she said with a smirk.

"What are you talking about?" Lil Hak looked very confused.

"Oh, your dumber than you look. Some dude named Lez put a hundred and fifty-thousand dollars on your head a few days ago. It's all over the town. Shit, I heard about it in the club." She smirked, thinking of what she was about to do with all that money.

"So, you're gonna kill me for a hundred and fifty-k?"

"You damn right. I got kids, nigga. Plus, you just played me like a dumb bitch," she yelled, hyping herself up to kill him.

"You are a dumb bitch," Lil Hak said laughing.

"What the fuck you say," she said, placing her index finger on the trigger.

"First of all, you not gonna kill me." Lil Hak walked towards his nightstand, slowly, so she wouldn't shoot.

"Don't fucking pull no funny shit. I'll blow your dick off," she said.

"Relax. I'm getting this." Lil Hak picked up his clip and she had no clue what the fuck it was as she looked dumb.

"What's that?" she asked, feeling something wasn't right.

"You can't shoot me without bullets," Lil Hak says, walking towards her.

The lady pulled the trigger, but there was only a click. She pulled it twice more to get the same reaction.

"Dumb bitch."

"I was playing around. I would never hurt you, baby," she said, trying to back paddle out the door but Lil Hak punched her in the face, knocking her into his room wall.

The gun fell and he picked it up, placing the clip inside and cocking the gun. "Somebody sent you?" he asked her, seeing how scared she really was.

"No, I swear. I just wanted to build with you. I never thought about killing you until you kicked me out," she said, begging for her life.

"I believe you, girl."

"So, can I leave? I swear this will never leave your crib," she told him, thinking about her kids.

"That's not going to happen today," Lil Hak said before he pulled the trigger, hitting her in the chest three times, thinking what he should do with the body. Lil Hak took his bed sheets and wrapped her up inside like rolling a blunt. "Stupid bitch," Lil Hak said getting dressed so he could take her dead body across town and toss it over the bridge into the river because he wasn't in the mood to do anything else, especially digging some fucking hole in the dirt somewhere.

***

DARBY, PA

Lil Jet just got done putting his son to sleep and he was tired himself, but he knew Beth would be coming in any minute from her morning run. Life was good for Lil Jet, but the only problem was he wasn't used to the quiet life, ducked off in some middle-class area. Every day he missed the crazy street life, but for many reasons he didn't miss seeing niggas like Lil Bean and Big Lack die. That shit hit him hard. At times he wanted to get back in the field, but there was no need to. He had money saved and Beth opened a nail salon. Income was steady and good, but he missed the fast life, the dangerous money, the blood money.

Looking at his son, he smiled knowing life couldn't be better for him to be free and alive. He talked to Lil Hak and a few other Sosa Gang niggas from time to time, but it was pointless because every conversation would lead to him wanting to go backwards. Lil Jet sat on the living room couch wondering what was going on with Sosa and Twin because nobody seen them in a while. Deep down he knew niggas would always look at him different from falling back and wanting to be a family man, but a real friend would understand.

CHAPTER 4
SOUTH PHILLY

Dirty hopped out the luxury car in Saigon Projects where he was raised and grew up. His hood was one of the toughest Projects in south Philly and he had much love for it. The Outlaws used to have a stronghold of Saigon Projects until Crispy got killed a while back by his new ops, the Sosa Gang. Now his Projects was mainly the D.C. Crew and he was expanding them all over the city, getting their name back up and running.

Since his cousin Wayne was killed in the club by the Sosa Gang, he was left to take over the crew. Dirty was living in Atlanta when Wayne came home and started fucking with them Sosa Gang niggas. Dirty remembered telling Roddy before he got killed not to trust them, especially Lez or Lil Hak. He knew personally.

The city been kinda quiet lately since the death of Kane from the Outlaws. It seemed as if everybody vanished, but that was perfect for him and his crew. Dirty came back to Philly and came up on a plug and turned up certain blocks in the city because it was a drought in Philly. At the moment, the coke and dope prices were rising.

He walked into one of the buildings and entered the trap house his bulls was getting more out of. "Ashy and Doty," Dirty yelled for his two shooters and capos of the crew he formed in the last month.

The trap was filled with guns, money, drugs, and bottles of liquor. Four young bulls were shooting dice in the corner, paying the boss man no mind.

"Dirty, what's up, ski?" Lil Ego said with his loud, annoying voice.

"Y'all fools shoot dice all day. Y'all should be out there getting money, not losing it to each other," Dirty told them, seeing close to twenty bands on the floor.

"We letting Lil Pete and X5 hold down the Projects. They had been stepping their game up out here, bull," says Ashy coming out the back with a blunt of weed hanging from his fat lips.

"Where your black, dirty ass been at, cuz? I was calling you all last night," Dirty said to his childhood.

"Nigga, I caught a DWI. This dumb ass nigga Doty came to bail me out drunk and he got booked up with me, trying argue with police."

"Oh, yeah?" Dirty laughed, knowing how crazy his crew was.

"Lil Ego and JT came to get us and shit. I'm still mad," Ashy said looking at niggas shoot dice.

"Where Doty at anyway? I need that two hundred-k," Dirty stated.

"He at his BM crib."

"Hell nah. I ain't going over there. That bitch crazy. The last time I went to get him, she pulled out a gun on me, bro. I told Doty that crazy bitch got one more time and I'ma kill her myself," Dirty said.

"Shit, she shot at me twice, bro. The first time she said I looked like a nigga who shot at her when she was in Iraq. Bro, look at me. I'm black as hell," Ashy said as Dirty laughed, knowing how crazy Doty's baby mother was after doing 10 years in the army.

"I gotta go, so hit me later." Dirty was about to leave until he saw Doty's tall ass walk right inside with a bookbag.

"What you doing here, bro?" Doty said looking drunk still from last night when they went out to party.

"I came to collect."

"Here. It's all there, cuz, but this goofy nigga got me booked last night." Doty looked at Ashy, shaking his head, peeping the dice game going on, about to hop in the mix of it.

"Nigga, you should've sent JT down there. You know he don't drink," Ashy replied.

"Next time, your ass staying in there. I'm still on parole," Doty said.

"Y'all should get married," Dirty said.

"Fuck you, nigga, but I heard somebody saw that nigga Twin today in 5th street Projects," Doty said.

"He's back, huh?" Dirty said.

"So I heard, but I told niggas next time anybody see the young bull, call me so we can take care of that," Doty replied walking off to the dice game.

"Keep your eyes open, cuz. Them Sosa Gang niggas may have something up their sleeve. They had been gone too long," Dirty placed the bag over his shoulder.

"Iight, that's a bet. I'm already on it," Ashy assured him.

***

SOUTHWEST, PHILLY

Imam Ahmad had security all in his Mosque now because he felt it was well needed. Since exposing his true identity to Twin, Rizzy, and Foxy he felt safety was a must. Being a kingpin plug and the leader of the Outlaws carried a lot of weight, but there was no hard burden. Then, being one of the most knowledgeable Imams in the city and a cold-blooded killer. Living a double life for so long, he got used to it, but he never felt right about it because his heart was pure for his Islamic religion, but his intention was another. Supplying Kane was a mistake, but he had to use him for the time being until he felt like it would be safe to show his face which is now.

Having Janasia, the head DEA, by his side was a blessing because they had been getting away with murder and so much more for a long time. The only roadblock to their success was the Sosa Gang. Having Twin kidnapped was his plan just so he could spare his son because Twin would be a good plug to what he was trying to rebuild.

For years he let Sin, Crispy, and OG Kane run the show, but that shit was over. Imam Ahmad had big plans to take over the tri-state and every hood in Philly.

Growing up in poverty and coming from nothing made him want to take control and build his own foundation, so he did. Around the same era the Junior Mafia was running the streets, he used to be down with them and cop weight from some of their close peers. He had been wanting on his son to come see him with an answer for 30 days now— if Twin would be joining the Outlaws or becoming a target for them. Imam Ahmad gave Twin the option of coming to his side of dying with his gang. He gave Twin 72 hours to make that choice and he haven't heard a thing, so Imam Ahmad made his son a marked man. He always prayed that it would never come down to this, but it was the game and he had to protect what he worked so hard for, and he would die before anybody would come close to taking what he worked his life away for. Imam Ahmad read his Islamic books and relaxed until prayer time.

CHAPTER 5
Miami, FL

South Beach on a Saturday evening was always packed and filled with people coming out for a summer or tanning. Barry had his lawn chair and beach towel in the sand with is feet out, rocking a bucket hat and sunglasses. Moving to Miami turned out to be helpful and smart on his behalf, especially after what the fuck been going on in Philly. Barry had a condo in New York, Texas, LA, and Miami for years but never really used them, instead kept them as safe homes.

Things in Philly got nasty so fast Barry had no choice but to run because he knew the police, Feds, DEA, and local drug law enforcements were all coming. When he got the heads up, he left, but the news of Elina being one of the main federal agents fucked him up. The whole time with Elina he never once saw any type of flaw that would have led him to believe she was building a case on him. That wasn't the icing on the cake for Barry. It was when he found out his ex-wife was out of the mental hospital and wanted by the FBI also.

With Ashley out, this could be the beginning of something big, and she would do anything to kill him. The history between him and Ashley went deeper than anyone could imagine. In the start of their relationship Ashley started to supply him— that's how they met. Before Barry fell in love with her, she was already a known killer and one of the biggest coke dealers on the east coast. Ashley showed Barry how to get money and move up in the game because he used to be green as grass. Once they started having kids, their life changed for worst. Ashley tried to live a regular life and enter motherhood by birthing their kids with Barry. Ashley wasn't happy and Barry knew this. He saw the look on her face every day. When Ashely ran off, he wasn't surprised at all. The only thing that hurt was who she went back to which was her ex-boyfriend— a Colombian kingpin nigga.

Left to raise two boys and a daughter, he took upon that duty and did what he had to do for them. He eventually found a good plug and locked down the city of brotherly love, but the only issue was the Outlaws, mainly Imam Ahamd. Not too many people knew

35

Imam Ahmad was deep or even in the game because of his position within the community as a righteous leader. Barry been made plans to retire, but not like this on the run.

Every month he planned to come up with a plan to skip state to state just in case the Feds were close, but this wasn't his first time on the run. Years before his kids, he beat two Fed bodies in New Jersey when he was out there moving big weight in Newark. He knew what the Feds had on him now would finish his whole career and he couldn't go out like that. At the age he was at, Barry regretted a lot of things— selling drugs, and killing was one. Barry wished he could've lived a square life and worked a nine to five like a regular joker, but growing up, his mom always used to tell him he wasn't normal.

***

DOWNTOWN PHILLY

Janasia sat at her desk in the DEA office thinking of how one of the biggest cases in Philly was slowly going down the drain, and she found it strange. When she got the news about Wayne's death it put a big dent in her plans because he was a top person on her list. The shocker was when she heard about Kane's body being found that really hurt the case, especially for the FBI, even though she was the killer.

Being a top Outlaw member wasn't easy trying to live a double life especially as a DEA agent. She knew it would be hard to put her double life together outside looking in, so she kept a distant from the organization. Janasia flipped through the documents on her desk of Barry and Ashely. She was really amazed by Ashley's story because the woman ran a drug circle from a nut house. Wondering where Ashely was hiding out would be too much of a headache, but she had a plan to at least fish and that's where Sosa would come in.

Sosa did a great job at ducking big cases and she couldn't help but figure out how he could shake every indictment. He had to have something going on with someone in the high position because it wasn't that much luck on earth

One person who haven't left her mind in a long time is Lez. He was laying low like most of the Sosa Gang and she found this very strange, at least knowing how they were. Deep down she had a feeling something big was about to happen soon and it would expose a lot of things.

***

TEMPLE UNIVERSITY, PHILLY

Zarhya recently came back to school after almost losing her life to the hands of her boyfriend at the time, Rizzy. She became stronger and was mentally prepared to go up against anything. The hardest part was coming back to school after what happened to her on campus. The whole school knew about it because it made the news. If it wasn't for her friend, she may not be alive today. Rizzy had been playing her the whole time because when she woke up from her coma, she easily put everything together, and Rizzy must've had beef with her brother Sosa. The small scar on her face will always be a memory of what she had been through that day, but Zarhya was really grateful to be here.

She was walking to her class when a friend named Toya stopped her next to the restroom. "Hey, Zarhya, I'm so glad you're okay," Toya said, giving her a hug.

"I'm good. What's up with you?"

"Work and school. Same thing. The school stepped up security on campus after what happened to you. Everybody thought you was dead," Toya told her, happy Zarhya pulled through because she really liked her.

"Thanks for the flowers. That made me happy."

"No problem. I gotta go. Call me." Toya walked off as Zarhya went to use the restroom before her class.

Romell Tukes

CHAPTER 6
DELAWARE, DOVER

Lez stood in the trap house as his cousin QB cooked the drugs he brought groom Philly this morning. Lez had been trying to stay out of Philly for a while because shit was crazy. After Sosa shot him, his whole outlook on the gang changed and the true love came out the bro's heart.

Lez knew from the look of shit the night at the airport with Foxy it could've been taken as a sign of disloyalty, but Lez was trying be smart. He didn't want Foxy to be tricked by her father so he felt the least he could do was put her on game. That night was the last time he saw Foxy. Lez hadn't heard anything about the Sosa Gang besides Lil Hak trying to lock down the city still, but everybody else went ghost and that made Lez a little worried.

Recently he found a new plug and had been fucking with his cousin QB who was getting big money in Delaware.

"This shit coming back good, cuz," QB said, sweating while whipping the coke like a pro on the stove.

"It's good coke, bro," Lez said, opening a bottle of Henny for himself.

"Facts, but you spending the night here?" QB asked because Lez had been spending a lot of time in Delaware.

"I'm straight. I gotta head back to the city, bro. I just wanted to make sure you was set with work."

"Aiight, but your hood still hot?"

"Not really, but I'm not trying get got lacking out there. Niggas moving real funny." Lez thought about his gang.

"I feel you, bro. That's why you gotta ride with a hundred shots," QB told him, seeing the product rock up.

"All I need is a thirty."

"Talk that talk then." QB laughed as he planned to cook up the rest of the nine keys on the table.

"I'm out. Hit me later. I'ma have my little homie come to pick up the money later, cuz." Lez walked out the crib that had a strong odor from cooking coke.

***

CHESTER PHILLY

On the outskirts of Philly was a small area called Chester. It was Rizzy's new stomping grounds where he had been moving a ton of weight. He got out the new Lexus to chop it up with his boy Roll who he had been rocking with for years now. With OG Kane out the way, Imam Ahmad was taking care of all drug transactions.

"Rizzy, what's up, bro?" Roll came out the lobby eating some cold fries with a big pistol poking out his side.

"Ain't shit. I heard y'all niggas blew a bag in the club last night in North Philly, young bull?" Rizzy asked.

"Bro, that shit was a movie, cuz. It was my cuz birthday," Roll said, checking across the street, seeing his workers selling all over the blocks.

"That's fair, bro. Y'all ain't invite me. That's crazy," Rizzy stated, leaning on the wall as his bust down watch shined from a mile away.

"We know the club ain't for you, bro." Roll knew Rizzy wasn't heavy on partying.

"I heard some Sosa Gang niggas were in there?"

"Hell yeah. They were fifty deep in that bitch, turned up." Roll remembered how the Sosa Gang niggas turned the club upside down. "The owner had to kick them out the strip club because they were slapping bitches and all." Roll shook his head.

"Dem little niggas most likely from southwest, down with Lil Hak because the rest of them been laying too low." Rizzy had been thinking about his ops lately because shit had been too quiet lately.

"You know these niggas?" Roll said as a Chevy pulled up, and then two niggas jumped out concealing weapons.

When Rizzy saw it was Lil Hak, he went for his burner, but the MP5 assault rifles went off.

Tat, Tat, Tat, Tat, Tat, Tat, Tat, Tat … Tat, Tat, Tat, Tat, Tat …

Rizzy saw Roll caught a headshot as he dipped into the building as Lil Hak and his goon cleared the block out in a matter of seconds.

***

Lil Hak and his young bull Don were spinning through the hood to see Don's cousin about some weed. When Lil Hak saw Rizzy, he wasn't about to miss the chance to leave him where he stood.

"We missed that nigga, cuz. I swear it's like them niggas got nine lives," Lil Hak said, upset he ain't get the chance to kill Rizzy.

"Y'all killed Sin and Crispy, so everybody else should easy because them two niggas were vicious," Don said, driving back to southwest with ten pounds of weed in the trunk.

"I think whoever up about to be worst because they had to kill Kane if we didn't, you dig?" Lil Hak knew the new Outlaws were worse than the last crew. When he heard Kane got murked, he knew they were coming back stronger, but he was ready. Lil Hak just wanted his crew back— all of them.

Romell Tukes

CHAPTER 7
UPTOWN PHILLY

"Ohhh, shit…" Allure moaned on all fours, taking every inch of Sosa.

Sosa came to her crib this morning and they had been fucking since he entered.

"Yesss, zaddyyy, fuck me," she screamed as he spread her ass cheeks to go deeper into her soaked coochie.

"You miss this dick, huh," Sosa said, trying to hold his nut.

"Uhmmmm." She bit her lips, yanking the sheets and almost ripping them off the bed, loving all of him.

Sosa missed his girl, but there was something he needed to figure out with her because his mom put her out there and it's been bothering him.

"I'm cumming! Oh my God…!" she yelled, rubbing her clit as she creamed all over his cock, making her sex more gushy.

Sosa nutted in her seconds later before pulling out, feeling drained.

"That was amazing. I missed you so much, baby. Where you been at? It's been almost two fucking months," Allure said, getting dressed because she had a photoshoot for a magazine in Texas.

"I had to take care of something out of town. I'm sorry, boo."

"So, you leave for two months then pop up on me, fuck the shit out of me, and think nothing about it. I missed you every day. I thought something happened to you. I lost my father and got into a bad car accident," she stated sadly, thinking about OG Kane, her dad, who the police found murdered floating in a river.

"I'm sorry, baby. Come here." Sosa grabbed her arm, looking at her sexy body.

"You're gonna leave again?" She sat in his lap.

"No, baby. I had to take care of something important."

"You sure, baby?" She looked him in the eyes for truthfulness.

"Yes. I'm all yours, Allure, but how come I never met your mom or dad?" he asked as she got up to do her hair and finish getting dressed.

"Oh, I forgot, but you never asked." She tried to beat around the question, hoping he would change the subject.

"Well, I would like to meet your family." Sosa saw how uncomfortable she was.

"I don't really have a lot of family, Sean. My dad got killed, my brother I ain't even know got killed, and the rest of my family is in Cuba on my mom's side," she said.

"Iight, baby. Whenever you make time."

"When can I meet your family?" she shot back.

"Soon, hopefully." He smiled, getting out of his bed to prepare for his manhunt on Barry.

"Okay, can't wait." She went to the restroom.

***

Chestnut Hill Philly

Vera lived in an upscale area. Her mansion was the biggest on the block and she lived there alone with five bathrooms, seven bedrooms, two levels, indoor pool, and a large backyard. Her alarm clock woke Vera up at 6AM as it did every morning so she could get her dog started. Vera's regular day was coffee, exercise in her gym, shower, then check on her investments, mainly real estate in York and Philly that she recently opened.

The last two months she had been very hacked dealing with Barry vanishing, Kane's death, and also the loss of her son before all of this. When she found out Kane killed her son Prince, he didn't know about things changing. Vera had her son Prince with Barry while Kane went to prison, but when Kane found out, he killed Prince the future of the NBA.

Vera planned to kill OG Kane herself, but someone beat her to the punch two months ago.

Kane left a lot of drugs in a stash house she only knew about. Vera's plans were simple: find some soldiers to move the shit, and go back home to see her family. In Cuba, Vera's brother was a big-time coke supplier, maybe the biggest kingpin in Cuba at the moment. She had been watching a few people in Philly who would be a good choice for the line of work she had up her sleeve.

***

WEST PHILLY

Foxy drove through her old hood in a new all-white Range. She had a few blocks back up and running after the Sosa Gang niggas basically shut her shit down, making the block hotter than fish grease after back-to-back shootouts.

With her dad dead things had been a lot better and smoother for the Outlaws. Imam Ahmad was good on drug transactions, so she never had problems. Foxy had a big crew of chicks getting money for her all over the city and the outskirts also.

Sosa Gang niggas been out the picture which was surprising to her, but they were still around. Every now and then Lez would cross her mind and how he took a bullet for her against his own crew. Even though he saved her, she still knew he had something to do with her brother Dawgy's death, so shit would never be the same.

Romell Tukes

CHAPTER 8
WEST PHILLY

Foxy got a good parking spot next to Overbrook to meet up with Queeny, a young woman who was moving products for her and doing a great job. She popped her trunk, grabbed the Louis Vuitton shopping bag, and walked slowly across the street, stopping traffic. She looked so good.

Soon she would need some product within the next few days because the coke was so pure the customers always came back for more.

Foxy stressed to her workers they should sell the pies whole or at the least break it down into ounces, but never should they be on the block selling hand to hand because that caused too much attention.

As she walked in the apartment building, the thought of Janansia popped up in her head. She really disliked her, and at any chance she would kill her for the slightest thing.

Seeing her and Imam Ahmad kill her dad hurt just for the fact she wanted to do it herself .

Foxy knocked on the apartment door taking off her shades, hearing chains unlock and the door open.

"Hey, bitch" Queeny let her inside.

"You been in the gym?" Foxy said seeing Queeny lost a little weight.

"Nah, but I started a new diet, though, and it's working," she bragged, turning around, showing off her new figure.

"Everything is in order, right?" Foxy said, placing the Louis Vuitton bag in the kitchen as two other women were placing money in a money-counter, counting stacks of paper which was a week's income.

"Yeah, girl. You know how we do. They about finished, but what'cha got for me?" Queeny looked towards the designer shopping bag, seeing it was looking real heavy.

"Thirty-four."

"Bricks?"

"Nah, dicks," Foxy shot back, showing her what was inside the bag.

"Okay, let's get it, then. I need me a new truck anyway," Queeny said, seeing her girls were done with everything.

"I'ma be back in like a week with some more. I just gotta take care of some shit," Foxy told her, putting all the bricks on the kitchen table so she could fill the shopping with the money.

"Be safe," says Queeny.

"Fuck being safe . I'ma stay dangerous. Bitch, believe that." Foxy smiled, leaving to take the money to the stash house.

***

DOWNTOWN PHILLY

Elina arrived at the federal building minutes ago to start her day at work. She went into the break room to make herself a cup of coffee which always helped her get energized. Since her big case went downhill her boss placed her at the desk and off the field. The Barry, Wayne, Kane, and Ashley case crumbled so quick before her eyes she couldn't believe it.

Wayne ended up murdered in a club in Philly which put big a dent in the case because her boss knew he had something to do with the Sosa Gang which could've been a bigger case. When OG Kane's body was found in the river, the city's biggest rat, that faded any hopes of taking down the city and cleaning it up. Barry went off the radar and so did Ashley which was shocking because the FBI had people working at the mental hospital to watch over her. Elina heard Ashley was mentally fucked up, so for her to be to escape a high-security mental hospital was impossible.

"Good morning, Maura," one of her coworkers called Elina by her real name because Elina was her work name.

"Hey, Limb."

"How do you like sitting at the desk doing paperwork?" Agent Limb joked on her because everybody knew how much she loved to be in the midst of the action.

"How do you like sucking the boss' dick and drinking his cum every day?" she shot back.

"Not as much as you love your decreasing career." He laughed at her, leaving Elina alone.

She walked to her small station, seeing a few of her co-workers loving the sight of her lows. When she took the case and had to play as a lawyer and Barry's girlfriend to hide who she was, it took a lot of work. Everyday she thought if Barry would find out what he would do because she knew how dangerous he could be. Warning Sosa was a big risk, but she felt like it was the right thing to do because he was a good kid. She also really liked him. The day he fucked her in the lawyer office was the best quickie she ever had in her life.There wasn't a day that went by where she didn't think of him, but he and his whole crew went ghost. She found this odd, but deep down she felt some shit was about to go down.

Romell Tukes

CHAPTER 9
NORTH PHILLY

It just hit midnight and three luxury cars with HD headlights pulled into the back of Malcom X Park for the first Sosa Gang meeting in a few months. Everybody climbed out the cars with a whole lotta ice on their wrists and necks, looking like made men.

"What's up, young bulls?" Lil Hak said, happy to see his guys all here except for Lez.

"Where Lil Jet?" Sosa asked.

"I spoke to him and he really out the game; trying to take care of his seed and Beth." Twin stated.

"I respect that, bro," says Lil Hak, knowing how much loyalty he put into the gang; even Beth who crossed sides and helped them.

"That's good, bull. I'm happy for him. Some of us can get out, but some can't, and I'm the one who can't," Sosa added.

"Facts, bro." Lil Hak felt the same way.

"Lil Hak, you been missing in action, so I'ma update you first on Lez. He a op. Now that you know, but Twin was kidnapped by the Outlaws," Sosa said.

"No shit, bull no wonder why I ain't see you," Lil Hak stated.

"Yeah, man. My dad was the main leader, him and the DEA bitch Janasia. I couldn't believe it, bro. I watched them kill Kane like it was nothing," Twin added.

"I thought that nigga was Foxy dad or some shit?" Lil Hak was confused.

"He was, but she was there at the meeting with the Rizzy, bull, and watched him kill her own dad. I couldn't believe it," Twin said.

"She must've knew he was a rat," Sosa stated.

"Maybe, but when my dad gave me seventy-two hours to pick between y'all or to join them, deep down my mind was already made up, bro." Twin knew he could never turn on his gang just to spare his life; he believed in honor before death. He also knew his dad will have more respect for him standing on what he believed in as he taught him.

"What we doing now?" Lil Hak wanted to know because he needed some product. Shit was still booming in Southwest.

"We back, cuz, with a new plug. The first drop off will be here in a few days," Sosa said, ready to get back to a bag.

Sosa spoke to his mom the other day on a pay phone and told her Barry was hiding. She told him cool; she would find out where he's hiding because she knew him very well. Ashley wasn't gonna make him wait on the product so she told him a load will be coming this weekend to, but he still owed her.

"That's a blessing, cuz, and we still got all of our blocks," Lil Hak said.

"I heard something about Dirty trying take over some blocks in West and South Philly," says Twin.

"Since Wayne's death, the D.C. Crew been getting their numbers up, bro. We gotta watch them, too," Lil Hak says.

"We gotta get him out the way," Sosa said.

"I agree, but until then, let's get back to this paper. I'ma hold down Southwest and the West," Lil Hak said, taking Lez's area since he wasn't Sosa Gang no more.

"Iight. Hold down South and North, plus Northeast. It's some homies over there," say Twin.

"That's said and done, cuz." Sosa was glad everything worked out. His only concern was all their ops raising, trying to take the game out.Sosa had to pay someone a visit to give his appreciation to them because if it wasn't for her, he wouldn't be here right now getting shit back in order.

***

SANTA CLARA, CUBA

Sebastian and his men waited in his large backyard filled with flowers and a view of the mountains in the background. He loved coming in his backyard to get some fresh air because he lived a hacked life. Sebastian controlled a big portion of drugs leaving Cuba from the coke to heroin he sold all over the world. The drug game wasn't his dream as a kid. He wanted to be a doctor, but his parents had a different dream for him and that was to take over the family business.

At eighteen years old Sebastain was already killing other Cuban kingpins and moving drugs in the States and other small countries like Haiti and Dominican Republic. Sebastian had two sisters, Giuliana and Vera, who both lived in the States, and now Vera was coming to get product daily, trying to take over Philly, she told him.

Their parents were retired and living a good life in Miami. He would go see them every once in a while, but they stayed out of his business lifestyle. They gave him the game already, so now it was his time to do what they did but better.

Vera would be on her way any minute from the airport for the meeting to discuss a better way to get the drugs in the States because the last shipment got picked up by the FBI.

CHAPTER 10
SANTA CLARA, CUBA

Vera arrived in Cuba to meet with her brother Sebastain and talk about business with him. Things had been going well for Vera since the loss of her son Prince who got killed by Kane, the love of her life.

When Vera did her own little research to find out her husband was the reason for Prince's death, she plotted out Kane's murder, slowly, but it wasn't fast enough. The day she heard the news about Kane's body being found, Vera regretted not making her move sooner because she wanted him to die at her hands.

She had been selling weight in towns like York, Allentown, and Lewisburg but she had been keeping her eyes on a young man in Philly. She wanted him to work for her, but she was gonna wait until the right time.

Two trucks escorted her to Sebastain's crib. She texted her daughter Allure who was in Philly with her boyfriend. Allure had been so busy with her career and life that they hadn't really had a lot of quality time to spend with each other, but she was gonna soon make that all up to her when she got back.

The truck parked in the driveway, and she got out feeling the humidity she hated because it made her skin sticky. She walked into the mansion like she owned it and went to the backyard where he was always was relaxing. "Sebastain, what the hell you been up to, bastard?"

"You look like you up to no good," he told her, knowing she was up to no good all the time, even as a kid.

"All the time."

"How's business going for you in the States, sis?" he asked, already knowing how business was because she was re-ing up daily.

"The coke is on point, but you need to lower these prices. I'm coping a hundred at a time." She made a point.

"I know, but the coke is going to be high for a while."

"Why?"

"Cuban law enforcement have been warring with us lately and shit, so we been in a bad position," he told her, pouring himself a glass of liquor.

"You need to take care of that because I ain't gonna keep paying these high ass prices," she told him.

"I'ma handle it. I promise."

"Good, but Kane got killed a few months ago. He killed my son. That fucker lucky they got to him before me," Vera said.

"Kane was good people. Why would he do that, Vera?"

"Jealous and envy."

"How's my beautiful niece Allure? You have not brought her out to see me in a while. Is she okay?"

"Modeling. Running around."

"That's good. Tell her to stop by some time. I miss her."

"Will do, but when will you be ready for me, because I'm running low, and I got a new plot that will help us expand. It's just about timing," she said, not trying to give up too much detail.

"Tomorrow everything will be in order for you."

"Are you positive?"

"Yes, so you should just stay for a night and relax," he told her because she was always on the move.

"I got shit to do, Sebastian. I can't sit on my ass like a king. Sorry. I have to grind for it."

"You heard from mom and dad?" he asked.

"No, why."

"It's mommy's birthday today, and I'm sure she'll love to hear from you," he said, already knowing her reply.

"Tell her happy birthday and to choke and die on some cake or an AIDs dick," Vera said, grabbing her purse to leave for her flight. Vera hated their parents because they left Sebastain their empire and didn't leave shit for her or Giuliana.

Sebastain knew Vera had hard feelings about his position, but he was the only male and his people thought he would be the best fit to run the operations.

***

NORTH PHILLY

Lez was looking for a new crib in a decent part of North Philly to move out his old area because too many people knew about his hideout. Lately Lez had been plotting to really get back in the game and kill Sosa and whoever else was with him and he knew that would be the whole gang. If Lez had a block in Philly, he could start to build his own team but that would be a death wish.

Teaming up with the Outlaws was out the question. He didn't trust Foxy or none of them for that matter. He needed his own army, and he knew the right person who would be down.

He saw an apartment building that was brand new and looking for renters, so he pulled over and wrote down the number to see a text pop across his screen from Foxy. He had no clue what she wanted, and he wasn't in the mood to text back right now, so he went to go get some Philly cheese steak.

Romell Tukes

CHAPTER 11
CHESTER, PHILLY

Rizzy and his boy Quan were in a store talking about an issue that had recently happened in the hood.

"Rizzy, them niggas pulled up like twenty deep, and stripped four of our workers and took their packs, telling them to get off the block," Quan said.

"Where was you at?"

"In Jersey, cuz. I told you my girl got pregnant out there and wanted to have a one on one," Quan responded.

"I wonder who it was."

"Dirty."

"Who the fuck is that?" Rizzy asked; never heard of him.

"He from the D.C. Crew. Dude really dangerous, bro."

"The D.C. Crew? What the fuck is they doing out here?" Rizzy was confused.

"I don't know, but he must know it's some money out here and trying get his feet wet."

"That's not happening at all, bro. So this is what we gonna do. Load up some niggas and find out where he at." Rizzy ain't like to feel like he was being punked, even though nobody knew he was the man behind the mirror.

"We already found out, bro."

"Iight, so we gonna slide tonight on him and his crew."

"Bet. I'ma call you when it gets dark out," Quan stated.

"Do that." Rizzy walked to his car as Imam Ahmad called his phone which was a big surprise because the last time heard from him was at the meeting. "Holla," Rizzy answered.

"You okay, young brother?" Imam Ahmad asked, sounding like a proud father.

"Yes. I'm just taking it day by day. What do I owe this surprise to?" Rizzy asked, feeling it was a reason to his call.

"I want to speak to you."

"When?"

"This weekend if you can," Imam Ahmad stated.

"Okay, no problem. Just send me a location and I'm there." Rizzy couldn't figure out what it was about, but he hoped he wasn't about to be the next Kane. Unlike Kane, he wasn't a rat, so he knew it had to be something else.

"Sounds good," Imam Ahmad said before he hung up.

Rizzy got in his car and pulled off, going to prepare for later mission.

***

SOUTH PHILLY

Hours later, Dirty and a few of his boys were in Saigon Projects chilling, talking about how much money they were getting. Dirty was networking, trying to take over South Philly, Chester, and other areas of the city to lock it down. Yesterday he stripped a few cats with hopes of running them off the block and he planned to check on the status tomorrow. He had plans to clean up the city and get rich, he just needed a real official plug.

"Dirty!" KD yelled, coming out one of the project buildings.

"Ayo, bull." Dirty was about to get a dice game started.

"Can I hold a few bands, please, and I'll pay you back," KD asked, who was Dirty's cousin.

"Nigga, you got a job?"

"Nah."

"So how you gonna pay me my money back then?"

"I'll get it to you eventually, bro, facts. Shit just all bad right now," KD admitted because he was late on rent.

The whole hood knew Dirty was getting money so they all were on his body and not afraid to ask him for shit.

"I'ma take your word, bro," Dirty said, digging into his pockets when he saw the two vans pull up. "Oh shit!" Dirty yelled, getting his gun out as shooters hopped out the van with assault rifles and ski masks on.

Tat, Tat, Tat, Tat, Tat, Tat, Tat, Tat, Tat, Tat, Tat …

Dirty's niggas got hit up as they got caught off guard, but Dirty was busting back.

Bloc, Bloc, Bloc, Bloc, Bloc …

Dirty hit two of the gunmen as he dipped off, seeing KD's head pop off like a balloon.

Tat, Tat, Tat, Tat, Tat, Tat …

Dirty made it inside the building without a nick or scratch on him as he went to stash his murder weapon in his homie's crib.

Police wasted no time in flooding the hood and asking questions about what just took place, but nobody said a thing.

***

SOUTHWEST PHILLY

Lil Hak was in the Benz SUV with his legs cocked open, getting his dick sucked by two bitches who were both cold blooded freaks. "Shit," he moaned as they shared his dick— one deep throating and the other one rubbing his balls. Lil Hak ain't have pleasure like this in a long time but he was grateful to have it today. He had his eyes closed, loving the way they were making him feel, then something told him to open his eyes. When Lil Hak saw one of the women pulling out a chrome metal object, he kicked both of them backwards and grabbed his 9-millimeter handgun.

Boc…Boc…

He shot one of the girls in her face, squirting blood all over the other one who looked frozen. "Now, who the fuck is dumb enough to send y'all to kill me, bitch?" he asked.

"Foxy sent us. I'm sorry, Lil Hak, but—"

Boc, Boc, Boc …

"Damn. Now, I gotta clean this shit up," Lil Hak said, pulling up his pants, mad he just fucked up his new truck. He swore to get Foxy back for the attempt on his life.

Romell Tukes

CHAPTER 12
MIAMI, FL

Barry was drinking his coffee, preparing for his early morning jog as he did every other day. Last night Barry had a hard time sleeping for some reason, but he figured it was a bad sleep. Living in Miami couldn't have been anything but sweet for him at any cost because he felt free from life, especially after spending most of his life hustling.

Selling drugs for decades could take a lot out of any person if they let it, and Barry let it suck the joy and happiness out of him at an early age. There were times he missed his children daily, especially Zarhya. He knew Sosa would be good regardless because of his strength and mind frame.

Barry couldn't believe Ashley, his ex-wife, was back on the scene. This could only mean one thing. Shit was about to go bad. Very bad. He hated Ashley's brother who lived in LA. The two of them had a real beef with each other since the beginning of time when they all were living out in Philly. Barry gulped down the rest of his coffee and hit the exit, leaving his apartment, taking the stairs. He felt as if the elevator was for lazy people.

Once outside, the brisk morning air hit him hard but it wasn't too bad, and the sun was coming out so it would become a little warmer. Barry started his run up the block. Out of nowhere, two men jumped out from an alley, tackling him to the ground. Both men were twice his size.

"FBI! You're under arrest, Barry, for murder and drug trafficking," one of the federal agents said, placing cuffs on him quickly as four squad cars pulled up in all-black with tints.

Barry thought his life was flashing before his eyes as they tossed him in the backseat of the car, towing him off to the federal building.

***

MIAMI FEDERAL BUILD, MIAMI

"Barry, we got you— as they say in Philly— young bull," a tall white agent named Mr. Aston said, walking into the waiting room Barry was being held in cuffs.

"Let me call my lawyer," Barry stated seriously.

"Late, but right now, I need to know where the fuck is your ex-wife Ashley, because, to be honest, she is the one we really want, not you."

"I can't help you."

"Oh, no. Well, I bet when you get all this time you'll wish she was here with you. And let's be honest, do you really think Ashley's gonna keep you safe when it's her turn? Because trust me, we will get her smart ass, too." Agent Aston said.

"Sounds good, but I have no clue what you talking about," Barry told him.

"Okay, but do you know we got a recording of Ashley paying two dudes to kill you before she faked crazy? And she did a good job at that." The agent laughed, telling the truth because Barry had no clue what he was about to remain solid for which was a snake.

"Give me my lawyer call?" Barry wasn't trying to go back and forth, but deep down he knew the cop could be right about her trying to kill him.

"When we take you back to Philly, you can call the president if you want, but trust me, you're going away for a long time," Agent Aston guaranteed.

"Just like the white man hoping on a black man's downfall."

"Call it what you want, but if I could put all you black fuckers in jail, I wwould. Trust me," Agent Aston said, walking off as Barry tried to figure all this shit out. It was too much.

***

LOS ANGELES, CALI

Ashley took her private jet to LA so she could visit her brother Bless. Stepping off the jet in Jimmy Choo heels with a Birkin bag she saw Bless step outside of his Rolls Royce truck with three cars full of crips behind him as his security team.

Bless was one of the biggest drug suppliers in LA. He had the whole county under his wing. He sold meth, coke, dope, and weed to almost every main plug in the city. He was the nigga supplying them. Being related to Ashley was a curse and a blessing since a kid. She showed Bless the game and also put him on his feet before she took her break at the nut house.

"Come on, Ashley! I got shit to do! You taking yo' fucking time!" Bless shouted.

"Boy, hush."

"I see you traded in that straight jacket for a Louis Vuitton dress." He laughed at her. Bless knew what Ashley was up to in Atlanta because helped her come up with the plan to keep the Feds off her. One thing Bless knew was if the Feds got to her then they would soon be on him, so they came up with a quick plan that worked.

"Nice truck," she said, climbing in the passenger seat, loving the Cali heat.

"What's going on in Colombia, or wherever the fuck you be at?" Bless joked, pulling off on his way to his mansion in the Hollywood Hills.

"I'm happy to be back. I got your nephew Sean into the family business, now. I think he'll be a great asset," she said.

"I ain't even know you were back in business." Bless was shocked because he figured she would want to chill and live life.

"That's why I'm here, dummy. I want to be our plug again."

"You think that's smart? Hoping back in the game so fast with the Feds on you?" he wondered.

"I can't leave this game alone. This is all I know since I was twelve, Bless. You know this. It's all we have, so I won't let the Feds ruin my life, and they don't got shit on me," she said with an evil smile.

"My plug is the Mexican Cartel, Ashley, and you know how they are," Bless said knowing they wouldn't let him walk away alive.

"We kill 'em," she said as the SUV got silent for a second.

Romell Tukes

CHAPTER 13
DOWNTOWN PHILLY

Lez came out to a big event at the Convention Center; something he came out to every year. Coming outside wasn't his thing no more because the town was getting spooky and back dangerous, so Lez been extra on point. When he wasn't around, he would be out of town, getting to a bag. Tomorrow, he had a date with his plug, so he was excited about coping more work because he was seeing some big money out in Delaware.

"Lez ..."

He looked behind him and saw Foxy calling his name. Out of reaction he reached for his gun, thinking they were still at war, but he then remembered their last encounter with her at the airport. The last time he ran into Foxy was to warn his ex about her father, then Sosa rode up on them firing shots, shooting him. "Foxy, what's up?" Lez said, seeing she had on a Chanel jumpsuit.

"I haven't seen you in a while. Are you okay?" she asked nervously, seeing he was alone and not with Sosa Gang, but she heard the rumors of how they wanted him dead.

"I'm straight."

"Look, I really wanna thank you for—" Foxy saw him lift his hand up, cutting her off.

"You ain't gotta thank me, my nigga. We good, Foxy, but I gotta go. Take care," Lez said, walking off, leaving her standing there looking dumb.

Foxy felt so many emotions going through her stomach, but she knew they both crossed many lines in life. One thing she knew was when blood gets drawn, it's very hard to forgive. She watched Lez leave out the place. Deep down she wanted to follow him and beg for his forgiveness, but her pride and ego were too big.

"You ready, girl? We been looking for you," her friend Ree Ree said, pulling up with a fat ass.

"Oh, yeah. Let's go."

"Who was that fine ass, tall nigga I saw walking off?" Ree Ree asked, being nosy.

"An old friend," Foxy mumbled, thinking of a way to get her ex-lover back.

***

SOUTH PHILLY

Twin just coped an all-white BMW i8 with tints, stunting as he drove through South Philly to his Projects, letting niggas know he was back. Three days ago he flooded the hood with keys he got from Sosa and shit was moving fast because for the past month the streets had some bullshit work.

Sosa's gang was back to taking over Philly and Twin was stronger than ever. He parked in Wilson Projects, jumping out with two Desert Eagle handguns on him. A group of young niggas were outside admiring the car.

"What's going on, young bulls?" Twin embraced the whole gang.

"Out here pushing this work, trying get one of them joints," Massy said, pointing at the fly BMW coupe.

"One day you will. Just keep grinding. Every dog got their day," Twin said, entering the building to check on his cousin Trae B who was moving the drugs in the Projects for the crew.

Twin walked right into the crib to see niggas all over counting money, smoking weed, bagging up work, and Trae B was in the kitchen teaching a group of niggas how to cook coke without fucking it up.

"When y'all see this shit start to boil, it's cooking, but make sure it don't foam up and overlap the pot. You gotta keep the heat low once it starts to boil, and then you wait until you see a hole in the snow white. Then, you start to whip it. Don't let it stick to the pot. Put that wrist work in that fucker," Trae B said, whipping the coke, seeing Twin in the background listening to the chef. Trae B took a break and let one of the niggas fuck up a few grams of coke when tyring to cook.

"What you going to do? Open up your own cook shop?" Twin joked.

"Maybe. I gotta do something, bro. This shit don't last forever."
Trae B was a fat, overweight nigga, so he had to take a seat in the
living room which was dirty.

"Business is booming, bro," Twins says.

"Facts. That coke is different, cuz. It's like dog food."

"Damn, that's good," Twin said.

"What's up with your pops? I ain't seen him in the Mosque in
a while, bro," Trae B asked about his uncle Imam Ahmad.

"Bro, he a op. That nigga run the Outlaws. They kidnapped me
and all that."

"What? Ain't no way, bro." Trae B could not believe that because his uncle was a good Muslim man and an upstanding leader
in Philly.

"They got some real shit going on. A DEA bitch on their team
and all, bro. Shit real." Twin added.

"Damn. What you gonna do, though?" Trae B asked, down with
Twin regardless because he was the only nigga who held him down
when he went off to prison.

"It's litty, bro."

"Say no more, fam. We Sosa Gang at the end of the day," Trae
B said, rolling a blunt as Twin got out of there.

***

UPTOWN PHILLY

Sosa was in his crib about to take a shower. He was just waking
up from his nap because getting a good night sleep was rare these
days. He walked in his walk-in closet to see Allure's gym bag. He
peeped inside to see what was there and it was mostly photos. At
first, he was going to leave her shit alone to give her privacy but
when he saw the picture of her with OG Kane, he paused.

"How the fuck could I miss this?" Sosa said seeing a lot of pics
of Allure. He placed everything back in her bag before rushing in
the shower. He was thinking how could he sleep with enemy and
the thought of Allure knowing who he was hit his mind also. She
could be lining him up.

Romell Tukes

CHAPTER 14
NORTHEAST, PHILLY

Lil Jet came out of the house to pick up some diapers and baby food because he was running low. Beth was at home taking care of the baby on her day off of work today. Living like a square was starting to fuck with his mental. He missed the streets and the action.

He was also grateful to be alive and free so he could take care of his family. Lil Jet knew a lot of niggas who ain't make it to his age, so he was proud of himself. Not hearing from the gang in a while made him feel some type of way but he only hoped they were all safe and well.

Pulling into the shopping center in his Hellcat, the only parking spot was next to a Benz. After parking, he saw a nigga coming his way next to the Benz, which must have been his car.

"That's you, bro. You almost hit my shit," the man told Lil Jet with an attitude and staring at him.

"Maybe bro," Lil Jet says trying to keep his cool, but the dude's energy and vibe was off.

"Aight." The man looked at Lil Jet once more before getting in his car and pulling out.

Lil Jet went into the shopping center to ponder on what just happened in the parking lot. There was something very off about the nigga he saw but tried to focus on getting the shit for the baby as Beth called him on Facetime.

"What's up, Mami?"

"I'm Mami today," Beth said, smiling on Facetime.

"You always Mami, sexy. You must miss me already," he said walking to the baby area.

"Always."

"The baby up?"

"Nah, he sleep babe," Beth said sounding real relief.

"Okay, I'ma pay for this shit and get some gas. Then, I'ma be back. I love you," he said.

"Love you more," she said before hanging up.

Lil Jet paid for everything and left the store but as he carried the bag, there was something in his heart that didn't feel right.

Out of nowhere, shots rang out. That's when he saw the man who had a few words with him before he came in the store.

Bloc, Bloc, Bloc, Bloc, Bloc, Bloc ...

Two bullets dropped Lil Jet as the crowd of people ran off and so did the shooter, who was Dirty.

Lil Jet was losing a lot of blood as civilians called the police. Dirty raced off in his Benz. The ambulance came quickly because they were nearby. They arrived at the scene and rushed Lil Jet to the Temple Hospital.

***

DOWNTOWN PHILLY

The federal building was having a big meeting today. Seventy agents all gathered into the large conference room to listen and take notes as the Chief of the FBI lead the show.

Elina sat in the second row paying attention to what the new plan was to lock up Philly's most criminals killers and drug dealers.

"Gentlemen and lady, we finally got a hold of Barry. He is back in our custody, thanks to the hard work of Mrs. Maura and a few other agents. So, thank you." He looked at Elina to see her smile.

"No problem, it was easy," Elina said, making a few agents laugh.

"I'm pretty sure it wasn't but now we have bigger problems to worry about. His ex-wife, Ashley who escaped from a fucking nut house recently. We had our finest agents in there looking over her very close. I believe she had some inside help somehow because for her to be mentally fucked up after her husband death and plot some shit out like this, she needed help. I think her help was from our number two target Bless, her brother who is moving drugs in LA on the west. I got in contact with the agent out there and they can't get Bless for some reason. I'ma send some of you out to LA so y'all can go undercover because I don't like what I'm hearing. There is some fishy shit going on, " the Chief said.

"How many you sending out to LA boss?" A male agent raised his hand to ask.

"Maybe ten of the best but I'ma need most of our elite workers here. Ashley is connected to a member of the Sosa Gang, who has been hard to keep tabs on. We found out he was the son of Barry, and his mom is Ashley so that leaves us to believe he could be the one moving all the weight in Philly," he said.

Elina got uncomfortable as she took a sip of water thinking how Sosa would be having big problems soon. When the Chief got on anyone ass, he wouldn't stop until it was over, and he won.

"Sosa Gang and the Outlaws have been fucking up this city for the past couple of years in a way we've never seen before. We need to get them all off the street but with Kane dead, someone else has to take over the Outlaws for sure. We need to find out who," The chief of the FBI said as a rookie raised his hand.

"What about the D.C. Crew?" A new young black agent asked.

"Wayne is gone and rumors we have is Sosa Gang did it so this will blow up soon. I heard Dirty has took over and I been watching him for a while, but our main focus is Ashley, Bless, Sosa, his gang, the Outlaws, and whoever else came between them and us. Meeting over." The Chief left as Elina sat there for a minute thinking of what to do because Sosa was in trouble now.

Romell Tukes

CHAPTER 15
FDC, PHILLY

Barry was on his way to a visit, but he had no clue who was there to see him. He couldn't see how all these charges was applied to him because it was a lot of shit he didn't do. He saw his ex-wife all in his paperwork for a lot of vicious murders she did since a teen.

When he read the part about she wanted him dead and hired two killers to kill him, he couldn't believe it. At the same time, he didn't put nothing past her at all.

The other day, his lawyer came to see him with bad news talking about two more murders the Feds was hitting him with.

Walking to his visit, he saw a few young cats talking about the Sosa Gang and how they had the streets on lock. Barry thought about his son and his baby, Zarhya, who was still in college. He received a letter from her yesterday. Tears flooded his eyes when he read how disappointed she was in him, but she did acknowledge how much he meant to her still.

Everything was going downhill. When he found out about Elina being the main federal agent who was building the case, he felt betrayed and hurt.

Never in Barry's life would he imagine out of all people, Elina being an agent. He was nutting all down her throat and fucking her in the ass whenever he felt like. She was his personal sex slave.

Being a vet in the game, he always knew this day would come but it was how it would come.

"Barry, you're table six," a female correction officer said, knowing who the old man was because his face had been all over the news for the past few weeks.

"Thanks." He walked to table six to see Vera sitting there looking appealing in an all red designer outfit.

"Hey criminal," she said, showing her perfect smile.

"Hey evil, I'm surprised to see you here. You hoping on my downfall, huh?" Barry said, sitting down.

"How you holding up?"

"I'm great. I can't complain. I'm trying to make it through the hard part of this trial." He told her.

"I can't believe they caught up with you. I must say you had the longest run," she admitted remembering being younger and Barry had the streets on lock.

"Shit happens."

"I'ma be honest with you, Barry. There are times I hate you but as I grow up into a better woman, I learned you wasn't a real man so I couldn't treat you as such. When I told you about our son's death, your reaction let me know you would never change." Her words hit him hard.

"Your right, Vera. I've made poor sad decisions in my life, and I stared at myself in the mirror to feel ashamed. I loved Prince. I used to go see him play ball at his games and I knew he would've been something special," Barry told her.

"We can't go back in time, but I will never forgive Kane for what he did. The hurt part of it all is I couldn't kill him with my own hands," she admitted with a sadden tone in her voice.

"I wish I could've been killed him years ago but he's gone now and someone else took his position in the Outlaws." Barry informed Vera something she already knew of.

"Fuck them but I have to go. Do you need help with anything? I know some good lawyers."

"I'm okay, thank you."

"I respect how you held yourself down and ain't rat. That's why I'm here," she told him.

"Morals."

"Facts, but take care." Vera got up to leave.

On her way out, she signed out in the log book where she used a fake name that was on her fake ID. She came up to visit Barry, not because she missed him, but she wanted to read him and his conversation just in case it affected her. She would be able to peep it and drag it out of him.

Vera had big plans and a new plot to get her drugs moving through the city of Philly in a matter of time.

***

MEXICO CITY, MEXICO

Ashley and Bless both went out to Mexico to pay Bless' plug a visit so they could talk.

"You ready for this meeting today?" Ashley said as his plug's security drove them to his crib.

"Hell yeah, but this shit going to be hard to convince this nigga to cut off his plug and let you supply him," says Bless driving through Mexico's nice area.

"Let me handle that. I just need you to introduce us and watch your sister work," Ashley stated.

They pulled up in the mansion and climbed out the limousine before walking up the stairs.

Rico opened up the door for his guest to enter his place of peace.

"Bless, you bring a friend?" Rico said, who was a short man with bald head.

"Yes, this is my sister," Bless told him as they entered the crib.

"I don't do business with others, and you know this," Rico stated.

"This is strictly worth your while," Ashley stated.

"Is that right?" Rico looked her up and down.

"I have an empire and I would like to supply. I run a big organization in Colombia and I'm willing to give you lower prices than what you are getting them for now," Ashley told him.

"So you that chick from Colombia I been hearing about?" Rico looked at her, not knowing she was black.

"Yeah."

"I've heard a lot about you. Come to my office upstairs," Rico said hearing about Ashley for a long time and knew she would be good for business.

Romell Tukes

CHAPTER 16
NORTH, PHILLY

Vera and Allure went out to get some breakfast together because they hadn't caught up with each other in a few weeks.

"Hey, my beautiful daughter," Vera said, coming into the diner, taking off her shades and purse before sitting down and glancing around.

"You look nice and tan I see. Where you been at?" Allure haven't saw much of her mom since her father's death.

"I've been handling business but now that you're here, I want to speak to you about some things if you don't mind," Vera told her.

"Okay."

"I know who killed you father, Kane and you have a sister," Vera said as Allure's face remained strong.

"When did you find all this out?" She asked, taking a sip of orange juice.

"Recently, baby and I had no clue he had a daughter named Foxy from out here near West Philly."

"I'm not too surprised," Allure replied as she showed no emotion.

"Yeah, but the part that's going to fuck you up is who killed him," Vera stated as she dug in her purse to pull out a photo of the killer.

"I thought it was you at first, mom." Allure admitted because before her dad's murder she was moving funny.

"Oh no, baby. I loved your father with all my heart." Vera lied with a bold clean face.

"I could tell." Allure took the photo from her mom and stared at the picture thinking it was a joke.

"That's him, baby. He's a very dangerous man and he killed your father," Vera told her seeing the expression on Allure's face.

"Can't be," was all Allure could say at the moment.

"Yes it's him. His name is Sosa. He runs the Sosa Gang," Vera said.

"Mom, this is my fucking boyfriend."

"What?" She said, sounding shocked and appalled.

"This is Sean, mom," says Allure.

"Oh no, baby."

"I got to go." Allure got up and took her purse confused and lost after hearing her man killed her dad.

"Baby, don't say a word about this and you have to pick a side," Vera told her

"Pick a side?"

"Yes baby, this man could kill you next. I can protect you."

"Mom, I just need time to think and clear my head," Allure says.

"Be safe. Call me if you need me and stay away from him."

"Okay, mom."

"Love you baby" Vera got up to hug her daughter tightly with a smirk on her face.

"Love you too. I just got to clear my head."

"I know baby," Vera said watching Allure leave thinking about how smooth her plan was about to come together. Vera knew Allure was about to be a queen on the chessboard as she prepared for her next move.

***

DOWNTOWN PHILLY

Janasia walked into the DEA building where she worked in a new business suit with her briefcase looking more like a lawyer than anything. Last week, she got a new big promotion which called for her own office on the top floor next to her boss.

Lately, she had been having the most state convictions in the city. Her hard work had been acknowledged on many levels. Nobody would ever think she lives a dangerous double life outside of work, but she did. Janasia loved the power and say so she had in the Outlaws being the top member next to Imam Ahmad.

Since he was supplying the drugs, it was her job to cover his tracks and the organization, which was hard because now the FBI was in the picture. There wasn't nothing in her way right now besides Agent Maura and Janasia had to do something because the woman was growing closer to her, and the Outlaws. Janasia couldn't have that. It would ruin everything she'd been working so hard for over the past few years.

The problem with the Sosa Gang had been heavy on her mind especially since Imam Ahmad let his son, Twin walk away clean, which had to be the dumbest shit she ever seen. Janasia pressed Imam Ahmad about that, and his reaction was blank. All he said was Twin would come around.

Inside her office, all she thought about was hooking it up to make it look more of her style since she would be spending a lot of time in there.

Every day she thought about Lez and how he was doing out there because word on the street is his old crew wanted him dead. There was something about him that made her feel special. She knew Foxy had a thing for him but if ever given the chance he would be hers not because she disliked Foxy but because she was really into him.

***

SOUTH PHILLY

Twin stopped to get some gas on this nice Sunday afternoon at a nearby gas station before going to see Lil Hak in Southwest. On his way out the car, Twin realized he had a low tire on his rear end.

"Fuck, my nigga!" Twin shouted out loud to himself.

Lil Hak called his phone, and he picked up

"Ayo." Twin walked inside to get some gas.

"This nigga Lil Jet in the hospital, bro. I ain't even know until I called him, and Beth picked up," Lil Hak stated on the other end.

"Damn, cuz. We got to slide on him." Twin paid for the gas and went back outside to see a truck speed into the lot. The SUV looked familiar, but shit was happening so fast his mind couldn't wrap around the shit. When he saw Imam Ahmad jump out, Twin thought his father wanted to talk until he started blicking off shots towards him.

Boc... Boc... Boc... Boc... Boc... Boc... Boc... Boc... Boc...

Bullets bounced off the poles and garbage cans as Twin try to take cover, seeing cars back out of the gas station not trying to get hit or nothing.

"I told you to join me. Now I got to kill you!" Imam Ahmad yelled trying to take off his son's head.

Twin slid into the passenger door side before starting the car to pull off as his dad put bullets into the car door. Twin left his gun in his car, so he had no wins, but he sped out of the lot.

CHAPTER 17
TEMPLE HOSPITAL, PHILLY

Lil Hak arrived at the hospital before Twin, but he texted him telling him to meet with the guys up there. Trae B popped up and a few other Sosa Gang members to make sure Lil Jet was okay.

The hospital main entrance looked like the front of a project building in Southwest Philly right now.

Lil Hak was waiting on Beth to come out to let them know what's going on but something inside of him said Lez did it and if so, there will be a lot of bloodshed.

Beth came out through the double doors, seconds later, looking tired because she had been through this phase for a few days now. She was in and out of the hospital.

"He's okay," Beth said as Lil Hak and Trae B both looked relieved.

"Aight, what happened?" Lil Hak asked, hoping she knew something about the shooting that took place.

"He was out picking up some shit for the baby and someone just started shooting at him," Beth said.

"He knows who?" Trae B asked.

"Nah, he said he don't know but I will tell you this. They just woke up a sleeping bear," Beth says.

"I knew sooner or later he would come back out of his shell because he can't adapt to no square life," Lil Hak stated.

"I guess it is what it is," Beth said, placing her purse over her shoulder.

"Call me when he can get visits," Trae B said getting a text from Twin saying he needed to meet him at a spot they had in South Philly.

"The doctor said he'll be out in a few days, so I'll call when we get home," Beth told them before going back to Lil Jet's room where he was only allowed one visitor at a time.

Lil Hak looked at Trae B leaving going out the slide doors with his crew. He figured he'll call Sosa to put him on game but if it wasn't Lez then it had to be the Outlaws. Lil Jet would've knew their faces so Lil Hak didn't know what to think at all.

***

UPTOWN, PHILLY

Dirty got done talking with his boy, Taff about a plug he could cop from but Dirty really was planning on robbing the plug. Taff knew Dirty for years and giving a nigga like Dirty his plug will cut his water off and put his life in jeopardy. Dirty would eventually kill the plug and fuck up everything.

Walking across the street to his car, he knew a plan B was his only way out of this one.

A car came out of its parking spot and drove directly into Dirty as the woman was texting and driving.

BOOM …

Dirty got hit so hard he back peddled before hitting the pavement. The woman stopped and got out the car to see if she killed him.

"Oh, my God. Are you okay I'm so sorry," the beautiful woman said kneeling down as a group of civilians watched.

"I'm good," Dirty said. Seeing how beautiful she was made him forget about how hard the lady just hit him seconds ago.

"I'm sorry, what can I do to help you?" She asked as he slowly got up.

"Maybe, a date?" Dirty asked the sexy woman who had exotic features.

"Maybe no, but I got some better." She went to her car and handed him a bookbag.

"What this?"

"Please don't open it out here. All the instructions are inside the bag. You will understand," she said walking to her car, climbing inside to drive off.

Dirty felt his whole body hurt but he knew with some good sleep he'll be okay. When he got in his car, he saw the bag and looked inside to see ten bricks wrapped up in blue tape.

"What the fuck?" He said thinking the lady gave him the wrong bag or something. There was a note inside the bag, and he read it.

"I've been watching you Dirty and I want you to come work for me, please. It's worth it. I'm Vera and I have a lot more of coke. You will be very happy to come work for me. I'ma give you the ten pies for free. If you ready to get rich, call me in two days at 7 PM. We will meet and do business. My number is below …

Dirty couldn't believe what just happened. He knew she hit him on purpose now, but he felt something special about her. Dirty already made plans to deal with Vera in his head. Plus, he needed her.

Romell Tukes

CHAPTER 18
DARBY, PHILLY

Lil Jet was back home from the hospital yesterday and he'd been doing his own research on who shot him. It wouldn't disturb his sleep no more. The police questioned him about what happened the day he was shot in the hospital and Lil Jet kept it street, telling them nothing.

This morning while searching on the internet, he saw a photo of the nigga who shot him. Lil Jet saw the man was down with the D.C. Crew and his name was Dirty.

Beth heard of him but wasn't too familiar with the nigga and neither was Lil jet but now they had a start, a big one.

"You hungry baby?" Beth asked as she walked into the room.

"I just ate. Thanks," Lil Jet said seeing how beautiful she was after the baby. He loved everything about Beth. When he got hit up, she was right by his side.

"I'ma go feed the baby. Holla if you need me." Beth turned to walk out the bedroom.

"Baby, I really want to thank you for being here with me and holding me down. It says a lot," he told her.

"It's my job. You're a good man under all that evil shit." She laughed.

"You make me better." Lil Jet saw her smile and leave the room.

"He saw his phone and it was Sosa who been said he was coming by to check on him.

"What's up nigga? Where you at?" Li Jet asked.

"Outside. This a big ass crib," Sosa told him parking.

"Beth going to let you in," Lil jet said, hanging up and calling Beth so she could open the door.

Since leaving the hospital, Lil Jet's body had been sore especially after getting of them pain pills. Too much moving would take a lot out of him.

Sosa and Beth walked in the bedroom, laughing and talking. Sosa could tell when he first met Beth that she was perfect for his boy.

"Niggas hit you up good huh, little nigga?" Sosa saw his young bull all wrapped up and shit.

"I'm straight though, bull."

"My baby good but I'ma go take care of this baby." Beth suggested and leaving the room.

"I should've pulled up to the hospital. My bad, I been trying to figure some shit out bro. I been sleeping with the enemy," Sosa stated.

"You?"

"Allure is Kane's daughter and my mom said she is also the daughter of some powerful Colombians."

"Your mom?" What the fuck did I miss in this bitch?" Lil Jet asked.

"Too much, but don't let my small shit overwhelm you, bro. How do you feel?"

"I know who shot me, cuz." Lil Jet pulled out his phone to show Sosa the pic of Dirty.

"He must be down with the D.C. Crew." Sosa saw the area the picture of Dirty was taken at and it was the D.C. Crew's turf.

"Yeah, they call him Dirty. He must have took over for Wayne," Sosa stated, staring at the photo.

"Maybe, but he a dead man. When I heal up, I'm coming back."

"You coming back to the streets bro?" Sosa asked.

"I got to."

"You moving backwards, bull." Sosa did not want to see Lil Jet fail. He had a son now and was out the way.

"Niggas just shot me the fuck up. I ain't finna let that slide. I'm not pussy," Lil Jet said.

"What you feel in your heart, bro?" Sosa asked.

"I'm back."

"Aight when you heal up, we will take care of this nigga," Sosa said as his phone rang. It was Elina so he knew it had to be important.

"But love you bro"

"Love you too. I gotta go," Sosa told his boy before leaving.

***

UPTOWN, PHILLY

Elina waited for Sosa at a Burger King fast food spot to speak with him about the last meeting at her job. Now his name was out there, shit could go very wrong.

Sosa's car pulled up right into the driveway next to her. Elina's heart started to race at the thought of him. She got out and put on her windbreaker coat because it was a little chilly outside today.

"Hey Sean, thanks for coming out," she stated as her mind flashed to the time he was fucking her doggystyle.

"Haven't saw you since the news you hit me with."

"I know. I wish there could've been a different way to have avoided that sense of discomfort," she stated.

"It is what it is, but I tried to help you as much as possible," she told him.

"Thank you for that because I could've been like Barry right now."

"Your father was just hit with a few more bodies so he's gonna be gone for a while, Sean" she stated seeing him look saddened because regardless, Barry was still his father.

"I hope he be okay but what brings you to reach out and how did you get my number?"

"I'm a federal agent. I can get anything I want but you have a problem bigger than me and my reach," she said, taking a deep breath.

"More drama." Sosa could tell by the look on her face she was about to hit him with some deep shit.

"We had a federal meeting. Your name was brought up. Well, your whole crew. My boss is taking it upon himself to arrest y'all, especially knowing Ashley is your mom."

"Okay,"

"That's all you got to say?" She said seeing him walk off

"Oh yeah. Thanks beautiful," Sosa told her getting in his car and pulling off.

Romell Tukes

CHAPTER 19
NORTHEAST, PHILLY

Dirty called Vera and she told him to meet her behind an old warehouse that had been shut down for a few years now. He saw Vera smoking a cig next to the same car she hit him with, almost killing him. The thought of her being a plug would've never crossed his mind if she was by passing him. In a matter of two days, the product she gave him was gone and it was fire.

"Dirty, how you feel?" Vera said, looking at him, seeing he healed fast.

"Thankful, I'm alive. Seeing that you almost killed me."

"I had to make it look real. People are always watching, you know," Vera says with a laugh because she didn't mean to hit him so hard with her car.

"Facts but the shit you gave me was a hit."

"Was it?"

"Hell yeah and I want to do business with you," Dirty told her, seeing an awkward look appear on her face.

"Doing business with me is like selling your soul to the devil."

"I been sold my soul to that muthafucker but at least now I can get paid for it." He joked but was very serious about every word. When Dirty was a teenager, he sold his soul to the devil and hoped for riches and fame.

"Okay, I'ma give you a shot but if you fuck up or try to come for me, I'll feed you to some wild animal in the Philly Zoo and I mean that," Vera stated.

"I believe you."

"Hope you do because they don't call you Dirty for nothing."

"I'm loyal to those loyal to me, Vera. You're in good hands. I'm trying get to a bag."

"There is someone else I'm working with and the two of you together will be a strong force," she says.

"I like working alone," he told her

"I like sleep naked. Who gives a fuck? You work for me now, not you. Soon, I'ma link the both of you up." She didn't even wait for an answer, she just walked off.

"Hold on, what happened? I... I'ma text you in three days. Be ready." Vera got in the car driving off.

Dirty wondered who she planned to team him up with, but he wasn't feeling this shit at all.

***

BOGATA, COLOMBIA

Ashley and some of her security guards were on their way for a big cartel meeting with a few top cartel families from all over Central America. To be a black woman amongst a group of the world's most dangerous men from all races was hard, but she had something they all wanted.

Since she wasn't considered a cartel, she was an independent contractor with ties and connections. She had big plans for dealings with the top cartel families to expand because she already had Colombia under her authority. The top Mexican Cartels were all aboard. Now, she had to convince other families to join the cruise ship.

Sosa was doing good in Philly. He had been moving a lot of weight and she wanted to speak with her son about moving to New York and Miami to open shops. She even wanted Texas but the Mexican Cartel controlled those areas.

Ashley's daughter's birthday was coming and she sent Sosa a gift to give to her, hoping for a bond with Zarhya because they didn't have one.

***

SPRINGFIELD, PHILLY

Zarhya lived in a nice quiet area that she loved but being at school full time was heavy for her, leaving no time to party or have any type of self-reflection time. Today was her birthday and Sean was on his way to take her out so they could go grab a bite to eat.

She was looking back on a few months ago when she almost lost her life at the hands of her boyfriend, Rizzy. It took everything for her to get shit back on track in her life.

Zarhya heard someone beeping a horn, so she got up and ran outside already dressed in a Chanel outfit with six inch heels.

Opening the lobby door she saw, Sean standing next to a red Lambo with a red bow on the hood. Zarhya told him about this car for years. She always loved Lambos.

"Happy Birthday," he said, pulling out a box with a diamond choker necklace for her.

"Oh my God, what have you done?"

"This is from mommy, the car and I got you the necklace," he told her seeing her face look confused.

"Mommy?"

"Yes."

"How did she buy me a car?" She thought Ashley was still in a mental house, but she had no clue who her parents really were. She knew her dad was arrested for some serious shit, but she figured it was all lies and the Feds were hating because Barry was successful.

"There are a lot of things you don't know about mommy and daddy."

"Tell me."

"Right now, are you sure?"

"Yeah." She shot back

"Mommy and Daddy are kingpin and queenpins. They are into that type of shit you see in movies.

"Oh," Zarhya said, not so surprised at all.

"Let's go eat, birthday girl." Sosa threw her the car keys so she could drive her new car.

Romell Tukes

CHAPTER 20
DOWNTOWN, PHILLY

Janasia's boss, Mr. Sargavio called her into his office in the back for an unknown reason.

Today was a busy day. She had a load of work to do, and she put herself on a time deadline.

As she walked to her boss's office, she got a lot of dirty looks from a few of her coworkers.

Being so young, beautiful, and black made her white coworkers hate her fucking guts but if they knew she could have their whole family killed before dinner time, they would suck her dick.

"Boss, you wanted me?" She said, peeping her head into his office.

"Yeah, come inside, please, employee of the month." Mr. Sargavio really liked Janasia. She worked harder than anybody in the building and he loved that about her.

"How was your fishing trip?" She knew he went on fishing trips with his family almost every weekend.

"I caught a few big red Snappers, it wasn't so bad." He put his pen down leaning back.

"Seems fun."

"Always but I called to inform you about some cases we have to re-up on a few crews," he said.

"What crews?" She got a little uneasy with his request

"Well, the FBI contacted me about the D.C. Crew, Sosa Gang, and they believe someone else took OG Kane's spot in the Outlaws," Mr. Sargavio stated.

"No way." She looked shocked but was really nervous.

"Why you say that?" These street gangs are quick to replace their leaders," he told her.

"True but maybe they vanished after OG Kane's death because we haven't heard too much out of them since."

"That could be a factor," he said, taking heed.

"Who from the FBI is taking the case?" Janasia wanted to know because this was too close to home for her. It could become an issue.

"A woman named Maura from the Philly District," Mr. Sargavio says, looking through the folder.

"Who the fuck is that?"

"I heard she is a real ball buster and a pain in the ass. She got a hard-on or a wet pussy whatever rocks her boat, but she wants these Outlaws," he says.

"I'ma look into the case."

"Please do. I'ma give this shit to you because I got a lot of shit on my plate right now."

"You busy?" She joked, knowing he was fat and lazy.

"I'm going through a divorce," he told her

"Damn."

"Shit happens. I caught my wife sucking her personal trainer dick in our bed. His penis was so big that I thought that black bastard had three arms," her boss said as Janasia tried to hold in her laughs.

"I'ma get on this." She got up to leave taking the files.

"Thanks."

"I got you." Janasia left her boss over knowing this could be a big problem if she didn't handle it right. She knew soon that a plan will need to be put in order to cover her own ass.

***

SOUTHWEST, PHILLY

Lil Hak loved being on the block in the middle of action. This was where he wanted to die at. Tonight, niggas were out looking fresh to death in jewelry and designer gear about to go out dubbing.

A BMW with tints pulled up on the block and everybody was on it ready to light that shit up.

Lil Jet climbed out and everybody showed him love. No matter where a person was at in the city, if they were down with the Sosa Gang, they wouldn't hesitate to show each other love.

"What the fuck you doing out here, bro?" Lil Hak said drinking a pint of Lean mixed with Sprite.

"I'm back. Sosa ain't tell you, bull," says Lil Jet.

"Nah."

"Yep. I'm on my bullshit. The nigga who hit me was from the D.C. Crew," Lil Jet stated.

"You sure?"

"Facts. His name is Dirty." Lil Jet hated even thinking about him.

"I heard of him. I think the bull from South Philly."

"Yeah, that's him."

"Say no more. We gonna lay on him but Beth let you out, huh?"

"She okay with it."

"You trying to party tonight?" Lil Hak asked knowing he ain't been out in months.

"Hell yeah."

"We about to slide in a few," Lil Hak told him.

"Bet." Lil Jet was happy to get out the house.

Romell Tukes

CHAPTER 21
NORTH PHILLY

Dirty arrived at 7th Cumberland to wait on Vera people that she told him about last night. He had no clue who he was here to meet but he saw nobody as Dirty climbed out the truck. Money'd been coming crazy for Dirty. He couldn't believe it. The shit he was getting was uncut and raw.

A pickup truck pulled up and a tall nigga hoped out and Dirty ain't realize who it was until he got close.

"You Vera people?" Dirty asked Lez who had no clue who he would be meeting neither.

Vera called Lez and told him to meet up with a new member of the team. She had been supplying Lez since he left the Sosa Gang. They met one night at a food spot and shit went to a business level. Lez thought it wouldn't be smart to set up shop in Philly, at least for now. Vera gave him the idea to set up shop out of town just until they built a crew.

Lez knew Dirty had to be her idea and plan for a new crew. The two men knew of each other but never had a face to face.

"This can't be," Lez says

"It is what it is. I could be here blaming you for my cousin Wayne's death but I'm not."

"You can't blame me for some shit I never did," Lez explained.

"It was your people, though."

"Fuck them bitch ass niggas. I run dolo."

"The streets talking, and I hear them niggas out for you," says Dirty already knowing about his beef.

"This ain't the first time niggas want me dead but soon you going to be a target, especially moving weight in North Philly," Lez stated.

"I guess word travels fast." Dirty knew the word of mouth would quickly sprawl about him getting rich and moving a lot of weight anywhere in the city.

"Facts."

"How you meet Vera?" Dirty asked because there was a lot of mystery to Vera, and he wanted to get whatever he could out of Lez about her.

"The same way you met her most likely. Fate or by chance," Lez told him, seeing someone was texting him.

Dirty thought he saw something move in the bushes next to a small wooded area connected to a building on the other side of the block.

Dirty pushed Lez on the floor saving his life as shots busted out from the shooter.

Boc, Boc, Boc, Boc, Boc…

Bloc, Bloc, Bloc, Bloc, Bloc…

"What the fuck?" Lez yelled getting his gun out while getting off the ground.

Dirty fired back, missing the shooter because of the dark area he was in.

Twin fired at Dirty hitting him once in the arm making Dirty drop his weapon on the ground as Lez picked it up and went to work.

Bloc, Bloc, Bloc, Bloc, Bloc …

"Ahh … bitch …" Trae B yelled, getting hit in his leg.

"Police!" Dirty yelled to Lez so they could get the fuck from out of there because nobody was trying to go to jail. Everybody went their own way avoiding any police contact.

***

SOUTH CENTRAL, CALI

Bless rode in the backseat of the Maybach looking out of the windows onto the tough blocks of Crenshaw where he was making a lot of money. Since his sister came back in the picture, he felt like his life been more stressful and all over the place.

Ashley had a way of working which was dangerous and deadly. She didn't give a fuck about life itself, so he knew his life didn't mean a thing to her. Blood or not.

Bless was on his way to check on the mother of his two kids so he could hit her off with some money.

Last week, Ashley started a war with a Mexican Cartel family with the help of his old plug, Rico. They started a big war, killing a cartel boss family in Mexico because he wouldn't cop from Ashley. Ashley was on some straight bullshit and she laughed when he recently told her about what she had been doing trying to turn everybody against each other.

Pulling into his baby mama's house, he saw her Benz that he bought for her last month as a birthday present. Walking inside, he saw the door was wide open which wasn't like Nekale. Once inside, he saw his baby mother dead on the couch with two bullets in her head. Bless couldn't even cry. He saw so much pain in his life. He walked out to go get his kids from the daycare center, knowing this was the Mexican Cartel's work.

Romell Tukes

CHAPTER 22
CHESTER, PHILLY

Rizzy had been shopping at Lowes department store for an hour to get shit for his new crib. He was hooking it up because he just moved inside two days ago. Everything been slow motion for him. The drugs he was moving in Chester was going fast so there wasn't any issues. He haven't been in the city of Philly too heavily because he didn't want to deal with the headache.

Pushing the cart full of home goods to his car, someone yelled out his name behind him. Looking back, he saw Foxy in a sexy Bodycon suit looking like some shit fresh out of a Phat Puff magazine.

"Hi Foxy," says Rizzy thinking about the last time he saw her at the meeting and how bad her attitude was.

"What you doing?" She asked, seeing his car full of supplies.

"I'm fixing up my new spot. I'm taking it slow, no complaints.

"I assume business is good out here for you."

"Somewhat but I'm waiting on Ahmad to hit me back on the next drop off." Rizzy had been calling Imam Ahmad for a couple of days trying to re-up.

"I've been waiting on him also," Foxy says seeing Rizzy had been in the gym lately because his chest was poking out.

"If I get a hold of him, I'll get at you," he told her.

"Rizzy, you got a girl?"

"Huh?" He was caught off guard by that comment.

"You heard me."

"Nah, I'm single now," says Rizzy thinking about his ex-girlfriend Zarhya he tried to kill but it went left.

"How about this weekend we go out for a dinner, on me?" She asked

"As friends, business partners, or just vibing?"

"Let's not put no label on it," Foxy told him before walking off.

Rizzy took a glance at her ass, and he knew she had some good pussy, just from her walk.

Rizzy did find her very sexy but her boujee attitude threw him off. He was turned off, but she really surprised him today. He couldn't wait to go out on their date to see who Foxy really was deep down. He had a feeling that she was wearing a mask due to her status in the Outlaws.

***

HOUSTON, TX

Allure came out to do a photoshoot for a mag that was making a big name for itself in the industry.

Vera recently gave Allure a choice to stick with her family or fuck with Sosa, who she claimed killed her dad, OG Kane. Allure made up her mind and she was standing with her man. Hearing Sean killed her dad crushed her heart. Never would she imagine the man she loved could take so much from her.

Every time she looked at her phone, it was a miss call or a text from Sean. Tonight, when she got back to the hotel, her plans was to block him from all social media platforms and change her phone number.

***

YORK, PA

Vera drove to her sister's crib to check on her because she called for two days and no answer. That made Vera feel something was wrong with Giuilana.

With Lez and Dirty on the squad, she knew soon a big chunk of Philly would be hers. When she zoomed her attention on Lez and Dirty, there was something about both men that made Vera want to work with them.

Now it seems as if her plot was slowly coming together, and nobody would even think she is running a drug ring because she was going to play it safe and low key.

Still doing the real estate on the side, she knew it would be best to continue a regular career with a legit background to protect herself from the law enforcement.

Her brother, Sebastian was loving Vera already because in the short amount of time, she was cleaning him out even though he grew the coke.

Pulling up to Giuliana's, she saw the car her sister drove and the cats in the living room window.

Vera wore heels so she walked on the wet grass, staying away from the rocky walkway.

Inside the house was cold with an odor as Vera made her was all the way inside and saw the reason.

She started to cry when seeing Giuliana laid out on the kitchen floor as cats licked her dead body. She was lying in a blood bath. There were so many bullets in her sister's body Vera couldn't even look no more. She walked out, thinking who did this.

Romell Tukes

CHAPTER 23
PHILLY, FDC

Sosa came out to see his dad, Barry in the jail today so he could hear what was going on. Sosa had recently killed Vera's sister, to send her a message because he knew what she was doing.

The past few weeks he had been keeping his eye on Lez and saw his connection with Vera, already knowing it had to be a money thing.

When he saw Lez and Dirty meet up, he called Twin and Trae B who was nearby anyway.

Sosa did more research on Vera and found out about her sister who lives in York. He'd been trying to contact Allure but there was something different about her.

Coming to see Barry took a lot out of him because he knew Barry was on the hot list and the feds would be watching all his moves.

Walking into the jail, he signed in the visit book and waited for his name.

After thirty minutes of waiting, his name was called for the visit. He walked into the visit room.

Sosa waited for close to an hour as his pops came down in the jail uniform.

"Sean, how you doing?" Barry said, sitting down with a bushy beard.

"I'm okay, just coming to see you and find out what's going on," Sosa said so much in such few words.

"Well, it's all bad."

"Damn."

"Yeah man, it's crazy. They just hit me with a few more murders that I ain't even do. Your mom did it," Barry said with a upset face.

When he heard about the murders, Barry knew off the rip who Ashley had to set him up or it was a mistake.

"You got a bail?"

"They denied me a while back." Barry shook his head.

"What's your plan?" Sosa knew his dad always had a backup plot.

"That's a good question man but I'm just going day for day, son. If I got to die in here, so be it. I lived my life," says Barry nonchalant.

"Have hope. I'ma do whatever I can to get you outta here. Just be patient," Sosa stated.

"One thing about Islam young bull is patience is a must in life," Barry told him.

"True."

"I wanted to tell you about Elina. She was a fucking FBI agent the whole time."

"You serious?" Sosa acted surprised and shocked.

"There is a strong chance she could be coming after you next. I want you to be aware," Barry told him.

"I hope she don't because I'ma kill that bitch."

"That's right, son. She's dangerous. I had no clue I was fucking the enemy," Barry said feeling like a loser. He was fucking Elina all those years and didn't have a clue.

"I got to go but I'ma look out for her."

"Do that. I'ma be okay, son. Just take care of your sister and watch out for Ashley. Your mom is probably trying to make some big moves while she's on the run."

"I'm on it, pops."

"Who you getting work from?" Barry asked as Sosa stood up to leave, not trying to speak on that.

"I will be back in a few months. Take care of yourself pops. Be safe," Sosa said leaving.

Barry realized how Sosa ain't say he loved him before he left out of the visit room.

Sitting there, a few ideas came to Barry's mind, but he knew who his real enemy was the FBI and Ashley.

He knew Sosa was copping weight from someone. He just hoped it wasn't Ashley or his son's life could be in some real danger.

***

BOGOTA, COLOMBIA

Sebastian just got done fucking his wife and putting her to sleep. They'd been married for a decade. Business been so heavy, he hadn't had any time to spend with his wife or kids. Today, he was gonna spend the whole day with them. Yesterday, he felt something was off and then he got the call from his sister, Vera about Giuliana's death. It made him emotionally disturbed.

He liked Giuliana more than he liked Vera because she had a good heart. Sebastian was gonna have his sister's body buried in Colombia where they were all born. He thought it was only right.

Vera kept her end of the business deal. As far as payments and shipment, she was on point. He went downstairs to his bar to pour himself a drink to relax his mind.

Romell Tukes

CHAPTER 24
SOUTH PHILLY

Trae B had been trying to get the money back he lost at the casino last week so he ain't left the trap in days.

"Trae!" His boy Scopy yelled from the backroom where he was laid up with a bitch.

"What, nigga. I'm bout drop off the quarter key across town." Trae B walked into the room.

"You trying drop off these two hundred grams to the nigga Wild and them on Southwest?" Scopy asked.

"Hell nah. Get your ass up and bust that move because you owe me money and I need all of that."

"Aight bro." Scopy pushed the woman off him.

"That bitch stank too, bro," Trae B said walking out.

"You gonna let him disrespect me like that?" She asked Scopy.

"Bitch shut up." Scopy got dressed and went to meet Trae B in the front of the crib.

***

Dirty and Lez both creeped through the hallway until they got to the door. Trae B was behind inside.

Earlier, one of Dirty cousins told him he overheard a nigga name Trae B talking shit about him outside.

Dirty's cousin gave him all the info he knew on Trae B and his trap house. Just so happened, Dirty saw Lez at a gas station and told him about the situation.

Lez wanted to slide with Dirty, so they were on their first mission.

Dirty gave Lez a look and the door got kicked out open. Both men rushed the crib with guns to see Scopy and Trae B in the living room counting money.

"Y'all niggas know what's up, bitch ass niggas. Give me that money," Lez said taking the money outta their hands. They couldn't believe it was Lez, a nigga they used to look up to.

"Lez, come on bro. We was cool," Trae said.

"Use to be bull. You a op now, bro," say Lez.

"I ain't never cross you, Lez. At least give me away out." Trae B says seeing Dirty laugh.

"Bull, when Sosa crossed me, so did you," Lez stated, pulling the trigger.

Boc, Boc, Boc, Boc, Boc, Boc, Boc, Boc …

Dirty saw Lez kill Trae B, so he aimed at Scopy, hitting him in the face dropping his heavy body.

"We suppose to shoot at the same time," Lez said.

"Nigga I ain't know when you was going to shoot." Dirty added

"You right, bro." Lez turned around to see a female coming out the backroom half naked.

Boc, Boc, Boc, Boc, Boc, Boc …

Dirty killed the woman, thinking she was a gunman about to hit him.

"Shoot first, ask questions later," Dirty said, seeing the woman's body slump on the wall in a sitting position.

**

DOWNTOWN PHILLY

It was 5 AM and the sun hadn't come yet as the darkness covered the sky.

Janasia came out to a high school track to go for a run in her jogging suit, but she wasn't only here to work out this morning.

A Cadillac truck arrived in the lot with HD lights. She stopped stretching and walked up to the driver's side.

"Get inside," Imam Ahmad told her as she climbed the passenger seat for their meeting.

"How you been doing?" She asked.

"I'm fine. Allah is the best of planners, Janasia."

"If you say so." She shot back not trying to get into the religion thing with him at 5 AM.

"The product got here last night. I'ma contact Foxy and Rizzy so they can do as they please."

"Cool, but we have an issue that can become big," Janasia stated, seeing cars pull up to the track.

"How bad is it?"

"FBI bad," she said as Imam Ahmad looked at her for the first time.

"What about them?"

"There is a woman trying to build a case on us due to the beef with the Sosa Gang and Kane's death," Janasia told him.

"Shit, I knew this shit would backfire." He spat.

"I'ma handle it. I just gotta look more into this agent bitch."

"You sure?"

"Yes, I'ma take care of it but we got to move smarter and not do too much out here. They gonna be watching and waiting." She told him.

"Okay."

"Call me when they get all of the product."

"Will do."

"Oh, what happened with your son?" She asked

"What son?" He gave her a look, letting Janasia know Twin was dead to him.

Romell Tukes

CHAPTER 25
DOWNTOWN PHILLY

Elina aka Agent Maura was going over the folder her boss dropped off to her this morning mainly about Bless and his old plug, Rico. There was also a few pages on Sosa and how he recently went to visit his father Barry, which just put the target on Sosa back. She spoke with her boss yesterday and he told her about a rookie agent he was going to have watching Sosa close to build a bigger, solid case on him. Elina knew how it was to be a young thirsty rookie agent trying to climb your way to the top.

Checking her lady Rolex, she got up to go find Sosa so she could tell him about the agent who was about to be on his line. She knew almost all of Sosa hang out spots in the city, so she planned to make a few stops.

***

NORTHEAST PHILLY

Sosa wanted to hit a gym in Fishtown today for some reason because he felt like he been losing weight. When he got the gym membership, the first month was constant but then Sosa fell off bad. Curling dumbbells was his favorite exercise because he wanted bigger arms and shoulders. Sosa was about to hit the jump rope when Elina walked in the gym on him as if she was gonna work out. He knew she had something else on her mind when Elina approached him looking sexy.

"Sean?"

"Maura or Elina?"

"Got jokes but I need to speak to you," she stated, grabbing some light dumbbells.

"Talk about it."

"You're in trouble."

"What's new? These days it seems trouble finds you when a person trying to stay out the way." Sosa looked at her

"Maybe."

"So, what is it now?"

"My boss wants you so bad. He just put a new agent onto you and he's thirsty," Elina says before curling the weights to make it look like she really came to the gym to exercise.

"You got a name?"

"Agent Hardy, a young white kid fresh out of college." She told him hoping Sosa didn't do no dumb shit.

"Okay," was all he said.

"So, you're going to chill now?" Elina wanted to know.

"This is my life, Elina but thanks. I'll forever owe you." Sosa got up to leave the gym.

Elina watched him leave, thinking what he was going to do because out of all people, she knew how smart and dangerous he could be.

She did a few more sets and got on the treadmill. She was in deep thought, hoping she did the right thing.

***

Agent Hardy was parked in a minivan watching Sosa come out of the gym. He leaned up in his seat. This was the second day he'd been on the case and knew it would be his big break and promotion. He wondered why Agent Maura came out to this gym out of all gyms in the city. Why come here was his mind frame.

Taking a few pictures of Sosa, he couldn't wait to nail him and his crew. Hardy was fresh outta college and the academy. He always wanted to be a cop since he was a kid.

His mom and dad both were retired cops in the suburbs where he grew up at. Being able to become a federal agent meant a lot instead of following his parents steps in becoming a regular cop. He watched Sosa drive out of his parking spot and made a quick decision to follow him so he could keep an eye on Sosa.

***

NORTH PHILLY

"Ohhhh shitt. Damn. Fuck that pussy!" Foxy screamed as Rizzy was deep between her legs, pounding out her coochie.

Foxy and Rizzy went out on a date, had a few drinks and minutes later, they were in a Hampton Inn hotel.

Her pussy was so good. Rizzy ain't want to climb out but he was on his nut.

"Fuckkk ..." She moaned, feeling his every stroke as he slowed it down to make love.

Rizzy couldn't fake the tightness. He nutted in the condom as he pulled out. She had juices pouring out her slit. Foxy started to make her way to his cock, crawling to the edge of the hotel bed. She eagerly wrapped her lips around his rod and sucked the tip. She was slowly going a little deep as Rizzy moaned, loving it as he got rock hard again. He stopped her and bent her over to fuck Foxy from behind. It only took a second for him to cum as she fucked the shit outta him all night.

Romell Tukes

CHAPTER 26
DARBY, PHILLY

Beth rocked her baby to sleep, singing a song as his eyes started to close slowly.

Taking the duty to be a mother was a big step in her life because she changed and matured in a small amount of time. The baby went to sleep so she placed him in the small carriage, wrapping his little body up nicely in the blanket comfortable.

She went into the living to check her phone to see if Lil Jet called but he didn't. Beth poured herself a drink and relaxed.

Since Lil Jet had been back in the field, she barely saw him unless he was going in and out the crib. The last time they had sex was three weeks ago. She was sexual frustrated and feeling down.

Being in the house all day would drive anyone crazy and it was starting to get in her head. When becoming pregnant, she never thought this how it would be. Stuck at home and raising a son while Lil Jet rip and run the streets.

Beth knew the streets and understood Lil Jet had to get revenge on the person who shot him but sometimes shit don't always turn out how people expect it. Sometimes the prey becomes the predator.

She wished Lil Jet was fully done with the streets and focused on raising his son like a man but deep down she knew he wasn't ready.

***

LA, CALI

Ashley wasn't able to sleep since arriving in LA at her new low key condo that she recently brought because she'd been spending a lot of time in LA with Bless. She saw the clock read 3:17 AM and there was no way going back to sleep was an option at this point.

Ashley had a lot of demands in life she lived with daily and only God could care for her soul.

Business was soaring through the roof as usual in Colombia and with local Cartel families, who were now purchasing from her because of her low prices and good quality.

While Barry is in jail, she could feel the law closing in on her, but she'd been using a dead person's identity for the time being to cover her tracks.

She didn't trust Barry one bit because he snaked her one too many times in the past. Ashley hoped he didn't brainwash Sosa into thinking she was this evil wicked witch from the east that will cross him because that was Barry's mind frame. Barry feared anything he couldn't control or use to his advantage.

Ashley went to wash her face and say a quick prayer before laying back down until she met up with Bless.

***

WILBURTON, DELAWARE

Lez had a SUV full of coke, pulling into the parking lot of a trailer park filled with mobile homes. The area was ran by his cousin, Hago, a dope boy and gunslinger, who knew how to get money.

With so much money in Delaware, Lez knew with the right plug, he could have it on lock in a short amount of time if done correctly. Teaming up with Dirty worked out perfectly. He liked the way he moved and handled his business with the gunplay and Dirty hustle.

Vera been keeping up to her part of the business arrangements and Lez really respected that about Vera. She wasn't all talk.

Hago walked out of one of the mobile homes with two white bitches. Both had phat asses and thick thighs like they were raised in the country.

Lez got out the car, laughing at his cousin's gold teeth because Hago was always talking about how he hated niggas with gold teeth.

"I see you, nigga. Out here looking like money with two bad white bitches," Lez joked, looking at both women blush.

"Nah cuz, they for you. I figure you may want to enjoy yourself for a second before sliding back to Philly." Hago had a deep voice that matched with his six-five frame.

"I got to pass bro but have them get that shit from under the spare tire out the trunk," Lez said as Hago gave his two white girls a head nod and they followed Lez's orders.

"It's a war out here, bro," Hago stated in a low voice so the women wouldn't hear them.

"With who?"

"Some New York cats who came out here recently trying to take over."

"You can handle it?"

"Facts, but I just wanted to tell you," Hago says.

"I know you can handle yourself but I got to slide. Call me later," Lez said leaving once the drugs were out.

Romell Tukes

CHAPTER 27
FORT WASHINGTON, PHILLY

Agent Hardy had a long day tailing Sosa around for almost the third week in a row but there was only one big issue. He couldn't find anything on Sosa. It was as if a life of crime didn't apply to him. Sosa was doing regular things normal people do like pay bills, go out to eat, drive around, go shopping, and hit the gym.

It confused him because from all the stories and files he read on the leader of Sosa Gang, anyone would think he lived a fast, wild, crazy life.

Hardy mom and dad cooked dinner tonight for their forty year anniversary. They had a nice large home on the outskirts of Philly where they lived in peace and quiet. He forgot to bring them a gift he had left at home, but Hardy knew his parents would be happy to see him.

Since working on the Sosa case, he hadn't been home to visit his parents. Growing up, they worked so hard that he barely saw them. His grandparents basically raised him.

As he walked into the house using his spare key, he could smell his mom's good cooking.

"Mom and Dad," he yelled, walking into the kitchen to see nobody.

When he turned into the dining room area, he froze after seeing his parents slumped on the tables and bleeding out of the holes in their heads.

"Hardy, you fucked up," Sosa said as he came out from the living room with Twin behind him.

"Sosa."

"You should of fall back," Twin says, looking at Hardy then his parents.

"I'm sorry. Please not my family. Noooo ..." Hardy cried.

"I've watched you follow me for weeks now," Sosa says

"It's my job but I have nothing on you," Hardy says, looking at his dead mother and father.

"Seems like you picked the wrong career, my friend," says Twin.

"You killed my mom and dad." Hardy was so stuck on what he saw. His mind couldn't see past anything else.

"In life, there are things we have to live with and do the right things for our future," Sosa said

"Man, what the fuck are you talking about?" Twin asked looking at Sosa.

"I don't know. I'm just trying to make it sound good before I kill a nigga," says Sosa before shrugging.

"Let's just handle this and go," Twin said, firing his weapon.

"Bloc, Bloc, Bloc, Bloc, Bloc, Bloc, Bloc, Bloc …

Agent Hardy's body collapsed onto the ground, and they walked out of the house, arguing about who wanted to take the final kill shot on Hardy.

Leaving the area, Sosa got a call from Allure asking to meet him somewhere so they could talk. Sosa dropped Twin off and made his way to the area Allure requested in the text.

On his way to Love Park, something in his heart told him that there was an odd energy he got from her. He put it in the back of his head.

Parking his car, he saw nobody, so he texted Allure asking where she was at. In seconds of waiting, he still saw nothing, which made him hop out of the car to get a quick stretch. Then, it happened.

Boc, Boc, Boc, Boc, Boc, Boc, Boc, Boc …

He saw Allure dressed in all black shooting wildly trying to chalk him out. Sosa was caught off guard as he climbed back into his car and drove off seeing she wasn't letting up.

Boc, Boc, Boc, Boc, Boc, Boc …

When Sosa got in a safe distance, he took a breath and saw a text from Allure saying she was gonna kill him and she hated his bitch ass.

Sosa now had another enemy that he had to watch out for, but he knew Allure like the back of his hands. It was her mom that he had worries about.

***

SOUTHWEST, PHILLY

Lil Jet and Lil Hak had been drinking all day in the hood, riding around on dirt bikes and turning up for Ressy Day, who was a Southwest legend.

Once a year, Bartrim celebrated Ressy Day in the hood by riding bikes, dice games, cook-outs, and drinking gallon after gallon.

Lil Jet had been in the hood so much that he forgot he even had a home to go back to with his family.

"What's good, Jet," Lil Hak said as he came from a drug deal he had just did in one of his buildings.

"About to hit Twin up. He still hurt over Trae B death."

"That shit fucked me up, bro. I really liked dude. He was solid," Lil Hak said, watching the bike stunts and picking up his cup of lean.

"I wonder who next," Lil Jet said as he continued to drink until midnight hours, thinking about Dirty.

Romell Tukes

CHAPTER 28
FCD, PHILLY

Barry had a legal visit this morning with his lawyer, Fairly, a white jew out of Philly. He was one of the best federal lawyers in the state of PA.

His other lawyer was on vacation somewhere on a boat enjoying his money, but he did his job.

Barry been past stressed due to his current situation. He was fighting a ton of bodies and drug charges. Most of his charges were based on Ashley.

"Mr. Fairly, thanks for coming out today. You got any news for me? Barry asked, sitting at the table in the jail lawyer room.

"If bad news is news to you, then I guess." Mr. Fairly opened up his briefcase, pulling out some papers. He had a look of disbelief on his face about the info he recently got.

"I'm not really understanding what you're trying to say."

"Oh, it's about to clear," his lawyer passed him a few sheets of legal paper.

"What is this?" Barry asked, reading something about Ashley but not really knowing what the big legal words meant.

"I don't know how this shit happened, Barry."

"Spit it out." Barry looked at the paper but not catching on to the legal language.

"Ashley's file has been dropped. She isn't a suspect no more and four more of her charges were placed on you. There will be a new formal accusation coming soon," his lawyer said.

Barry couldn't believe his ears on how Ashley could beat the system and fuck his life up.

"How the fuck is this possible?" Barry yelled.

"I have no clue. Either she knows some powerful people, or she is the daughter of Jesus Christ but whatever happened. You're fucked." Mr. Fairly was straight up with his clients.

"She is the reason why I'm here. She did all this shit not me!" Barry shouted as he got pissed off.

"Ashley is in the clear now. You got bigger shit to worry about."

"This fucked up. How the hell did she do it?" Barry asked himself.

"I don't know but I hope you know someone bigger than her you can rat on to get a lesser charge." Mr. Fairly told him.

"I'm no snitch."

"You better do something because I can't take this case. It will fuck up my career."

"Your career? I'm fighting for my life."

"We got two different lives, Barry. I ain't put you here. This what I'ma do. Either you can cooperate, or I can't be your lawyer, Barry."

"I paid you,"

"I will send your money to you in a check, subtracting the work I put in on motions and visits."

"Fuck you," says Barry getting up to leave. He was stressed out and pissed.

***

UPTOWN, PHILLY

Imam Ahmad had a doctor appointment with his doctor for his knee and lower back. Years ago, he got into a bad car crash on the highway with a eighteen wheeler.

A few days ago, he got all the product to his people and things were going good. Even though the problem with the Sosa Gang was starting to elevate in the streets.

He'd been looking for Twin all over the city but couldn't find him anywhere. Knowing the way his son thinks, Twin would let his pride overshadow his real inner thoughts.

Imam Ahmad remembered when he was a young man in the streets trying to build a name himself. He was dealing with the famous Black Mafia crew. Getting older in the game, he learned to play the background, run a Mosque, and let other people run his dirty work for him.

He walked into the doctor's office and signed in the book for visitors at the front desk.

Imam Ahmad saw a beautiful woman, who looked foreign, sitting alone in the corner reading a magazine. Trying to pay the woman no mind, he sat a few seats away from her. He was minding his business until someone said something. It was her.

"Richard Mille watches, nice," the woman stated, taking a quick glance at his ice.

"Thank you. Nice red bottoms," Imam Ahmad replied, looking at her heels and pretty feet.

"You must be a Muslim?"

"Yes I am," Imam Ahmad stated.

"I always been interested in Islam," she said as a doctor came out calling Vera.

"Maybe I can teach you."

"That will be good. Here is my card. Call me," Vera said, handing him her card and getting up for her doctor visit. As she was walking off, he looked at her phat ass.

Romell Tukes

CHAPTER 29
SANTA CLARA, CUBA

Sebastian stayed at his large mansion tonight while his wife went out on a trip with a few of her friends to Paris. He was sleep in his bed, getting a good night's sleep for his trip to Mexico tomorrow.

Sebastian woke up to take a piss in his private bathroom connected to the master bedroom. Climbing outta bed, he almost tilted over walking into the bathroom sleepy and turning on the light. Lifting up the toilet seat, he took a piss and heard the gun cock behind him. He pissed on the floor and was scared to death to turn around.

"Sebastian, you got a nice package down there, " a female voice stated behind him as she was up close.

"You making the worst choice of your life, " Sebastian spoke.

"Turn around so you can see who I am," the gun woman stated.

Sebastian turned around to see Ashley standing there in a hoodie and he knew it was all bad.

"Bitch."

"It's been long due, Sebastian. Facts," Ashley says.

"How long do you think after you kill me it will take my people to get your whole family?"

"You see Sebastian, I have no family, I'm all for us."

"Cold-blooded bitch."

"Something like that but at least you had a long, good run out here." Ashley had been keeping tabs on Sebastian for a long time.

"We could have did some good business together, Ashley."

"I realized you can't do business with everybody. That's when shit always go wrong," Ashley said then shot him five times in the face.

She walked out of the crib through the backdoor, the same way Ashley came inside.

She got a location on him from another Cuban family, who sold drugs and wanted him out of the way so they could have a strong hold over Cuba.

***

YORK, PA

Vera got a call from her cousin while she was showing a home buyer one of her homes.

Hearing Sebastian was found dead in his home fucked her up because she just got done grieving the death of her sister, Giuliana.

Trying to put the pieces together of all this shit was the hardest part but there was a connection somewhere. She just had to find it. There were a lot of people who could wanted to kill Sebastian because of who he was, but Giuliana was a different story. She lived a normal life.

Vera sat in her truck calling her baby girl Allure because she was all Vera had left in this cold, shady world.

Allure picked up on the third ring, happy to see it was her mother.

"Hey mommy," says Allure like a little kid who hasn't saw their mom in days.

"What's my baby doing?"

"In New York right now but I should be coming back to Philly in a couple of days. Is something wrong?" Allure could tell by her mom's voice something was wrong.

"Your Uncle Sebastian was killed last night."

"What, why?"

"I don't know but I want you home with me, baby," says Vera worried about her baby's safety.

"Okay, I'ma get on the first flight back home, mommy."

"Call me when your flight leaves, okay." Vera wanted to make sure Allure was well taken care of and the only way she could do that was by having her close.

Allure told Vera about her last encounter with Sosa, and she couldn't believe how tough her baby got to defend her mommy.

"I love you. I'ma finish up," Allure says

"Love you too." Vera hung up, seeing the couple who wanted to buy the house come outside talking.

***

SOUTHWEST, PHILLY

Lil Hak had just got done getting a quick blowjob by a chick named Karie from West Philly in his Range Rover.

"I love sucking your dick," says Karie.

"I love when you do it."

"Oh, the other day I saw your tall friend in North Philly chilling with that kid, Dirty. They must be getting some big money because North Philly looking worst then out here," Karie said, looking out the tints up and down the streets to see a few baseheads lurking.

Lil Hak could believe it, but he knew they were teaming up but to takeover North Philly was going to be a problem. He needed to call a meeting before shit got worst.

"Get out. I'll call you." Lil Hak kicked her out on the curb, pulling off to get up with Sosa.

Romell Tukes

CHAPTER 30
GALLERY MALL, PHILLY

Zarhya came out to pick up some clothes for tonight. She was going out with a few of her friends to a club for one of their birthdays. She been shopping all day. Her feet was starting to get hurt in heels, but this would be her last store.

Sosa called her last night to check on her, which was surprising because she barely saw him or heard from Sosa nowadays and it fucked with her.

Barry wrote her three days ago to let her know his situation worsened and he may be spending the rest of his natural life in prison. Zarhya didn't know how to react to the news. All she did was pray and try giving him support.

Hearing about her mom back in society somewhat rubbed the wrong emotions because growing up without a mother took a lot from Zarhya. She blamed Ashley for it.

At first, she was upset at Sosa for even taking gifts from her but one thing Zarhya knew is Sosa could forgive quick.

It would take years for Zarhya to forgive a person for small shit. So when it came to her mom, that hurt may lay on her Zarhya until she grows very old.

Zarhya had a new boyfriend named Miguel. He was a good dude, who worked at a warehouse. The thing she loved about her new man was the way he flooded her with love and care.

Her boyfriend called just as she thought of him.

"Babe ..." Zarhya answered happy walking around a store for some good perfume.

"I'm on break, baby. I just wanted to say I love you and check on you," her boyfriend said.

"That's sweet."

"You cooking tonight, sexy?"

"If you want me to," Zarhya replied.

"If you want to babe or I'll pick up some shit after work."

"Nah, I got it, baby. I'm headed home now. I don't have any school today so I'm not doing nothing," she replied, picking up a Gucci Guilty perfume bottle.

"Keep that pussy wet."

"It's always wet, daddy." she flirted back, not trying to talk to nasty in public because people were nosey.

When she hung up, Zarhya got two bottles of perfume. His and her for Miguel and her.

After paying for it, she left the store with her head inside the iPhone, reading a I love you from her boo.

Zarhya bumped into someone, almost dropping her phone and bags.

"I'm sorry I ain't –"

When she saw who it was, her body got numb. Fear took over her, staring the man who almost snatched Zarhya's life away.

"You look good, Zarhya," says Rizzy, staring at his ex-girl body and face, remembering all the fun he used to have with her before trying to kill Zarhya. He had to when he found out she was Sosa's sister.

Zarhya couldn't even talk when she was able to move. She speed walked off at a fast pace, not trying to look back. She was scared to death.

Rizzy stood there watching her leave as he wished they could fuck one last time. Even though his new girl, Foxy had some good pussy too, Zarhya's shit was on another level.

***

DOWNTOWN, PHILLY

The FBI building was having a small get together but with only a couple of agents.

"Someone is trying to obstruct this ongoing investigation. One of them goons as I call them has an obstinate determination to stop this case and we will find out. They murdered one of our agents and his whole family. Never in my life have I seen that happen so I'ma plagued and worried for all of our safety dealing with these lowlifes," Elina's boss said in a small conference room on the same floor as Elina's office.

"What's the plan?" one of the agents asked out loud.

"Me and Agent Maura will establish something shortly." The boss told all of them before sipping his coffee.

"Haven't she fucked up the case enough? We don't even have enough to get Ashley," a tall white agent stated, who hated on Elina for years because he wanted her position.

"If it wasn't for Agent Maura, we wouldn't have Barry or a lot of big cases so I'm curious to know what have you brought to the table beside dumb ass remarks." The boss shut him up quick as a few proxies laugh.

The meeting ended quickly, and Elina took a deep breath. She couldn't believe somebody from higher up was able to close Ashley's case. That put a big dent in her plans. Now, her boss would want to focus more on Sosa Gang and the Outlaws. She was already irritated. Shit wasn't going her way and Hardy's death made shit worse but she needed her own plan.

CHAPTER 31
DOWNTOWN PHILLY

The Sosa Gang all came out to a remote area for their meeting today. Lil Hak, Twin, Sosa, and Lil Jet got out of their cars dressed in black, not really knowing what the gathering was about.

"Since when we started coming out here, young bull?" Twin asked Sosa.

"This shit was Lil Hak's idea bro. Don't kill me, bro," Sosa replied.

"Let's start this shit," Lil Jet stated as a car's headlights could be seen pulling into lot with HD bright lights.

"Who the fuck is that?" Sosa asked.

"How the hell did she find me here," Lil Jet said approaching the luxury car as they all watched to see who was getting out of the whip.

"I thought I was down with the Sosa gang too," Beth said, getting out the car.

"Why are you here?" asked Lil Jet.

"I'm a part of this shit too," Beth stated waking up to them.

"What's up, Beth?" Sosa said.

"Hey guys." She greeted them all.

"Who watching the baby?" Lil Jet asked as he wondered how she even knew he was here with the gang.

"The babysitter, nigga. Now, what we on?" She asked, hopping up in the mix of things.

"I guess Beth back," says Twin.

"Well since we all here, let's get to it. Lez and Dirty has come together to go against us as we know but the question is how did they link up?" Lil Hak asked.

"Dirty?" says Beth, remembering his name.

"Yeah," Lil Jet stated never telling her who shot him.

"I know his baby mother. She used to dance," Beth said.

"You know where she lives?" Twin asked wishing they would have been knew this shit. The guys wouldn't be here right now.

"Yeah me and her cool," Beth said.

"Reach out to her," Sosa said.

"Okay, will do." Beth planned to hit her on social media later.

"The Feds are on us to now. Harder than ever before so I want us to be more cautious again," says Sosa

"After that Fed nigga you know they gonna be on us, cuz," Lil Jet said.

"That shit all over the news," says Beth, who'd been at home watching the local news daily.

"The objective is to avoid any confrontation with the law and when we go on drills let's just be smart," Twin said.

"Facts," Beth added.

"What the fuck you mean, facts? You not going on drills," Lil Jet told her.

"You don't tell me what to do," she shot back.

"Y'all need to take that Jerry Springer shit home," Sosa told them.

"He not coming home tonight. He's been staying with Lil Hak, so he's gonna keep his ass there." Beth's tone was serious.

"It's like that?" Lil Jet asked.

"Yep," she said

"Keep your eyes on the Outlaws also. They moving real low key. I haven't heard or seen Foxy or Rizzy lately. Janasia is another person," Twin said.

"And your dad." Lil Hak added.

"Facts," says Twin

"We know what needs to be done. Let's handle shit differently this time around," Sosa told them all before they wrapped up the meeting.

***

NORTHEAST PHILLY

Lez went into a fast food spot to order a salad and a bottle of water but this was to only get a clear look at the car that's been following him all through the city.

He knew the feds were in town, so Lez had been spending most of his days in Delaware trapping or fucking with Dirty.

Chilling with Dirty, he took a strong liking to him, and they built a sturdy bond in a short amount of time.

Looking out of the fast food restaurant, he looked at the black Toyota with tints parked up. Lez got his food and choose to pull a bold move, which was to approach the mysterious car.

Lez had his pistol on him just in case shit got hard and nasty outside on this wet day.

Lez walked right up to the car that had been following him. The tints were so dark he couldn't see who was inside. He knocked on the window.

When the window came down, he saw Janasia's beautiful face glowing.

"Why are you following me?" He asked.

"There is a lot going on right now and I wanted to catch you at a good time." She felt like a creep being caught tailing him.

"I already know what's going on."

"Yeah, but the law enforcements are all coming together to crack down on you and the ops." She told him.

"How the fuck did you become an Outlaw." He wanted to know.

"Next Saturday, come to this address and I'll explain," she said writing down an address.

"This may be a trap."

"That's my apartment address, asshole." She laughed.

"Aight, I'll be there," he told her leaving.

Romell Tukes

CHAPTER 32
NORTH PHILLY

Imam Ahmad woke up in a fancy hotel room from the long night he had with Vera, who was a tiger in bed and a super freak.

"I don't normally do shit like this but you're too sexy," he told Vera, lying next to her and seeing how beautiful she was fresh on a wake up.

"Shit, the way you handled me I can't really tell," she replied, rubbing his chest laying there wanting to cuddle with him.

"Baby, I don't cuddle or spoon so I'ma have to go." Imam Ahmad got up and climbed outta bed.

He ain't really know Vera like that but something deep down told him she may have hidden agendas. Last night, they had a nice dinner at the hotel restaurant near Temple University.

One thing led to another, and they went upstairs into a room and started kissing, touching, and fucking all over the room like savages. They knew very little about each other but that didn't stop the love connection they did have.

"Call me when you get a chance because I have shit to do also," Vera says getting out the bed.

"At least I can walk you to the car. I did have a good time last night, but I live a different type of lifestyle you may not be able to keep up with," he told her as they both got dressed.

"I hear you loud and clear, Ahmad. I'm sure we will meet again," Vera stated as they both walked out of the hotel room.

On the elevator ride, they both were in their own thoughts but still thinking about the best sex they had in a long time last night with each other.

"There is something about you, Ahmad," Vera says.

"I feel the same about you, beautiful," Imam Ahmad stated as walked out of the hotel lobby together side by side.

Walking into the parking lot, the sun was out beaming on them. Neither one of them was aware of the two men that hopped out with assault rifles in hand.

Tat, Tat, Tat, Tat, Tat, Tat, Tat, Tat, Tat, Tat, Tat, Tat, Tat …

Imam Ahmad and Vera both got low, pulling out their weapons and shooting back at the gunmen, whom Imam Ahmad knew.

"Come over here!" Vera yelled seeing the gunman trying to close in on Ahmad a few cars next to her.

Tat, Tat, Tat, Tat, Tat, Tat ...

Imam Ahmad looked Twin right in his eyes as his son tried to kill him. Vera tried to make her way to Ahmad until she got shot in the thigh.

"Ahhh fuck ..." Vera knee buckled but she never went down as Imam Ahman rushed to her aid.

Imam Ahmad was directly in front of his truck. He tossed Vera in the backseat as she dropped her gun.

Lil Jet fired into the SUV as Imam Ahmad rushed inside to the driver's seat driving off ,looking at his son one last time. He promises himself, Twin was good as dead.

"Shit it hurts ..." Vera moaned from the backseat.

Imam Ahmad knew a Muslim brother's wife who was a nurse and could help Vera get fixed up real quick.

"I got you; I know someone who can help you." He looked in the rearview mirror trying to stay within the speed limit, but something was bothering him.

"Thank you."

"Who the fuck are you?" Imam Ahmad wanted to know.

When he saw Vera shoot her gun, he knew off the rip she wasn't who his mind portrayed her to be because Vera was trying to kill something.

"I should be asking you the same thing," she shot back, holding her leg trying to stop the bleeding.

"We will get to that, but I saw you trying to save my life back there. Thank you," he says, pulling into Southwest Philly where his Muslim brother lived. His wife could help Vera's small problem.

"I think we both have some shit to come clean about," Vera said before Imam Ahmad parked and helped her out of the car, carrying her into the building.

***

WEST PHILLY

Aaliyah turned her crib into a small hair salon where she could make a little money at since quitting her last job at the hospital. Taking care of her two kids was hard. Especially with no type of help from her no good baby father, Dirty.

When she was in love with Dirty, he was a nobody. That's the reason they fell in love but the second she put him on his feet, things changed.

Luckily, she was able to make ends meet off doing hair but with two kids shit got real. With no help, it would weigh her down.

Today, one of her girls called to set up a hair date so Aaliyah cleaned up the shop while waiting on her friend.

The knock at the door made Aaliyah snap outta cleaning up the living room where she did hair at.

"Hey gurl," Aaliyah said opening the door for her friend Beth and some young handsome nigga she came with. It was odd because Beth used to always come alone or with Rika to get her hair did.

"You look good, bitch." Beth hugged Aaliyah whom she knew for years.

"Shit, thanks to the gym. I can't afford a tummy tuck." Aaliyah joked as they all walked into the clean apartment that had a hair chair in the living room.

"This is my boyfriend," Beth said as she introduced them.

"I'm Aaliyah."

"I'm Kevin."

"Gurl, he look good. God, oh mighty," Aaliyah whispered in Beth ear, always thinking she was gay.

"That's my boo." Beth gave Lil Jet a dirty look because they were really on bad terms, but they had to work together on this mission.

"Have a seat. I'ma go snatch up some combs and hair grease. What you was trying to get done?"

"Twists and braids to the back," says Beth.

"I gotcha. Make y'all self at home," Aaliyah told them before going to get her hair supplies.

"Aight." Lil Jet looked around liking what she did with the place, but he wasn't here to check out Aaliyah way of living.

"Let's make this shit quick," Beth said, pulling out a gun from her Chanel blue handbag.

"Chill out, I got this."

"Nigga you always wanna run shit," she told him.

"I'm not about to argue."

"I wouldn't even waste my breath on you." Beth rolled her eyes, putting her gun back in her purse.

"What the fuck is up with you, Beth." Lil Jet hadn't talked to Beth in days and they would have sex rarely. It was more like a fuck.

"Don't ask me no dumb shit like that," she told him.

"You really been acting like a bitch lately."

"A bitch? No, you're the bitch ass nigga," She said, hitting a nerve. Lil Jet jumped in her face but she ain't flinch one bit.

"Watch your fucking mouth." He yelled.

"Or what? You gonna hit your pregnant baby mother," she said revealing her new pregnancy status.

"Your pregnant?" He asked as Aaliyah came back.

"Is everything okay out here?" Aaliyah said as Lil Jet and Beth pulled out a gun on her to see her drop everything she had in her arms.

"Bitch, where is Dirty?" asked Lil Jet

"I don't talk to him, I swear," Aaliyah stated.

Boc, Boc, Boc, Boc, Boc, Boc...

Beth shot Aaliyah four times in the upper torso and twice in the neck, walking out and not trying to talk about the pregnancy no more. Lil Jet peeped game, so he left her alone for now.

CHAPTER 33
NORTHEAST, PHILLY

Dirty heard the news of Aaliyah's death minutes ago and had been fucked up since because she didn't deserve to die the way they did her.

There wasn't a doubt about who did this to his baby mother and soon, he would get the Sosa Gang back. The night was still young, so he poured himself up a pint of Lean to get his vibe right.

Lez was out in Delaware getting to a bag, but Dirty traps was doing numbers in the North and Northeast section.

"Dirty!" A nigga name Q Boy yelled as he pulled up to the block, getting out of the car as the shooters were on standby for Dirty.

"Q Boy, what's up bro? Welcome home, young bull." Dirty embraced Q Boy, who he did a few bids with back in the days before Q Boy did an eight flat.

Q Boy was from South Philly and lived a regular lifestyle, now trying to stay outta jail.

"Good looks, bro. I'm just out here working but I need to speak to you about a nigga named Twin," says Q Boy catching Dirty's look.

"Twin from the Sosa Gang?"

"Yeah, he fucking my baby mother. They been fucking since I was gone and me dude used to be cool."

"So, you want payback because he was digging your bitch back out?" Dirty laughed, knowing he was a tender dick nigga deep down.

"I mean y'all got beef, right?' Q Boy asked, trying to conceal his true motive for wanting Twin dead.

Since Q Boy was too scared to kill or go back to jail, he knew Dirty resume was all for the bullshit.

"He still fucking your BM?"

"Twin fucking her right now, bull. They in South Philly on Morris across the street from Papi store," Q Boy said.

Dirty walked off on Q Boy and got six of his boys and got inside of two cars, sliding to South Philly.

***

SOUTH PHILLY

Twin lost track of time as he'd been fucking Christina for the past two hours and a half nonstop.

"Damn Twin, my fucking pussy hurt babe. You do this to me every time," Christina spoke laying in the bed unable to move.

"You got that WAP." Twin joked, picking up his car keys to his Porsche.

"When you gonna get me a Porsche?" She asked as Twin turned around like he was an owl.

"Bitch I might not never," he told her leaving and seeing Sosa had been trying to call him the whole time.

Twin mind had been on a bag. The product Sosa was getting had south Philly going crazy.

"Ayo bull," Twin answered, walking out of Christina's apartment.

"Where you at?" Sosa asked.

"South Philly, nigga you know where I be at. What's up though?"

"I need to speak with you bro," Sosa told Twin just waking up from his cat nap at his crib.

"You home?"

"Where else I'ma be, cuz?" Twin walked out the building about to cross the street where his Porsche was parked up at.

"Call me when you outside," Sosa said, hanging up.

Boc, Boc, Boc, Boc, Boc, Boc, Boc, Boc, Boc, Boc …

Twin dropped to the floor, feeling a burning sensation in his right arm as he tried to crawl to safety while he was ambushed.

Gunshots was being fired from all over the streets as Twin pulled his gun out and shot two of the shooters who came with Dirty.

"It's over Twin!" Dirty yelled hiding behind a truck.

148

Boc, Boc, Boc ...

Twin arm felt like it was about to fall off as a Benz coupe pulled up to the middle of the block.

Everybody wondered who the fuck was dumb enough to pull up during a heated shootout in the middle of the street.

Beth jumped out with a military assault rifle. This was some shit a person could only get from the Marines.

Tat, Tat, Tat, Tat, Tat, Tat, Tat, Tat, Tat, Tat...

Even Dirty took off when he saw how Beth was knocking down his men like bowling balls.

Not trying to be next, he took off the same way he came. Twin saw it was Beth and made his way over to her, thinking where the fuck she came from. Beth saved his life because shit was getting real nasty.

"Thanks," Twin told her, getting inside his truck before the police came.

"I went to get some things for the baby and saw this commotion, but I'll see you next weekend for my birthday. We doing a cookout at my crib," she told Twin.

"Bet." He drove off, heading to Sosa's crib, thinking about Dirty bitch ass and running over a body.

Romell Tukes

CHAPTER 34
SPRINGFIELD, PHILLY

Foxy had a jacuzzi in the new home she recently purchased in a nice middle class suburb area where working white people mostly lived. Sitting in the jacuzzi , she was waiting on Rizzy to arrive with some weed and bottles of liquor so they could relax tonight.

Their relationship had gotten serious. She was already head over heels for Rizzy and his sex game drove her crazy. The only man she felt this way about was Lez and now Rizzy.

From time to time, Rizzy would pop up in her head, but she knew things could never be how they were, especially after Lez's crew killed her brother, Dawgy.

Rizzy walked into the bathroom where the jacuzzi was and placed the bag on the sink and started to strip.

"What are you doing?" She laughed at him.

"About to climb in with you!" Rizzy hoped she wasn't tripping because there were times where she would change up on him in seconds.

"Pour my cup first, nigga. You bugging," she said ready to drink.

"Okay, I got liquor and Moet?" Rizzy holds up both bottles.

"Moet, nigga. I'm classy," she says seeing Rizzy get a hardon from her naked body he was staring at.

"Oh yeah, I'ma fuck you good tonight." Rizzy rushed to pour the cups.

"I want it in the ass too baby," she said sexual as he got so nervous he spilled some Moet on the floor.

"You trying get crazy tonight."

"Facts, I can't wait until we go to Miami," says Foxy as they recently planned a trip to Miami to get out of Philly for a week soon.

"That's gonna be fun."

"I'll have the agency I use to book the flight and get the Air BNB house."

"Bet, baby. I just wanna spend some time with you on that phat ass," Rizzy said climbing into the warm jacuzzi water.

"You love me, don't you?" She asked looking into his eyes as he played in her tight pussy under the water.

"Hell yeah. You scooped me off my feet baby. The first time I saw you boo, all I could think about was you." Rizzy had never been in love with a woman. Foxy was his first. He valued who she really was deep down under the tough skin.

"I really love you."

"I love you a lot, baby and I don't never want this to end," he said, getting between her legs.

"Who says it does?" She replied kissing his lips as Rizzy entered her sex box which was natural tight and soaked. "Hmmm shit," she moaned as he pumped in and out of her slowly then picking up the pace going deeper.

Foxy and Rizzy fucked in the jacuzzi for an hour before they took it to the bedroom. She let him fuck her in the backdoor for the first time and she loved the feeling. The sex was amazing until they both caught cramps and passed out on the bed.

***

DOWNTOWN, PHILLY

It's been a busy week for the DEA office and Janasia been caught in the middle of all of it.

Janasia took on six new cases from the Badlands area in North Philly. Mainly, it was some Puerto Ricans who were known for drug running and murders.

The case was big, so she been working with her boss day and night to get shit underway for them to make out a warrant to arrest the Badlands crew.

"Janasia," her boss yelled from his office at 8 PM. Both of them were doing overtime.

"Yes, boss." She walked to his office.

"I just got a call and someone I've known for some time now, has some info on your guy," Mr. Sargavio stated

"Who?'

"Lez. One of my rats knows about two murders he committed," Mr. Sargavio said, getting up and grabbing his coat to leave.

"What's your rat name?" She wanted to know just in case she knew him.

"I can't tell you who my C.I. is, you might steal him. It's a cold game but I need you to drive me. My car is in the shop," he told her.

"Okay, sure, let me grab my keys." Janasia's mind couldn't stop racing thinking about Lez.

They drove on the highway outside of Philly. She had no clue where they were going.

"Pull over right quick so I can take a piss."

"On the highway?" Janasia asked, pulling over on the dark road.

"When you gotta go, you gotta go," Mr. Sargavio said, jumping out to take a urine in a ditch.

Janasia got out also and creeped up behind her boss. She shot him in the back of his head twice.

"I guess when you gotta go, you gotta go," she said herself, taking his phone and wallet out of his pockets. She was planning to toss it so it looked like a robbery.

Romell Tukes

CHAPTER 35
DEAR, DELAWARE

Sosa got another call from Elina asking him to meet up with her and since he went out to Delaware for a new car, Sosa told her to come out there.

Anytime he heard from Elina, in the back of his mind, he figured it would be most likely bad news.

The gang had been focusing on getting at Lez and Dirty because them two together could be a lot more good than bad.

In three days, he had to go out to see his mom in Colombia. Twin been collecting all the money for the last two days so everything could be in order before he flew out to see her.

He waited in a car dealership in his new Range Rover, finally seeing Elina's BMW truck arrive. He got out dripping in a Louis Vuitton jean coat and pants.

"Elina, what's up? You caught me off guard," Sosa said seeing how good she looked today in leggings that were showing her pussy print. Sosa couldn't forget the time he fucked her inside the lawyer office. She had the best pussy Sosa may have had in his whole life.

"Sosa, there is a lot going on and your name is being mentioned daily. What the fuck is going on?" She asked getting all up in his face.

"Elina, I been chilling lately. I don't know where you're getting your info from but that must be incorrect shit you getting," he told her.

"Sean, let's be real. You think I'm fucking dumb. I know about your beef with Lez and Dirty. They the hottest niggas in Philly right now." She looked him in his eyes, thinking how sexy he looks with his fresh shape up.

"Fuck them niggas."

"It's not about that."

"So, what's it's about Elina because I'm the one out here in the field every day." He explained to her, but she wasn't trying to hear shit.

"My boss thinks you and your crew killed the head DEA, Agent Sargavio, recently." She threw out there at him searching for details or any signs of guilt.

"Who the fuck is that?" He had no idea who she was talking about.

"Mr. Sargavio's body was found on the side of a highway by his co-worker, Mrs. Janasia." Elina saw the look on Sosa's face.

"Janasia, never heard of her." He lied thinking how this could easily turn into a big problem if not handled soon.

"You sure this is new to your ears because if y'all did this, I can't help you, Sosa."

"No, I didn't, Agent Maura. What else you want to know?" He got an attitude.

"Nothing else, I guess." She put her head down really wanting to say more but she chose to keep it to herself.

Sosa felt the vibe and leaned in to kiss her soft lips.

"I gotta go," he said, putting a spell on her as Elina's body locked up.

"Come by my crib, Sosa."

"When I get back from my trip," he told her, seeing the lust in Elina's eyes.

"You promise?"

"Yeah, keep my pussy wet."

"Always," she replied getting in her car and thinking how good the last sex session felt.

***

PEREIRA, COLOMBIA

Sosa's private jet his mom sent had just landed on time. He had two briefcases within the flight.

Since the news Elina dropped on him, he knew a plan had to be established someway, somehow. Luckily, he had a solid crew who told Sosa they would handle it for him while he was gone.

Another problem that was heavy on his thought process was Allure. The woman he figured would be his last, turned out to be an enemy this whole time. He had nobody to blame but himself for not seeing who she really was. It now affected him in the worst way. Having to kill someone you loved was a hard thing to live with, but Sosa'd been through this phase before.

Getting off the flight, he had on a Dior for men suit with sunglasses to block out the bright sun. There was a car awaiting him with two big bodyguards that his mom sent to protect her money, not him, whatsoever.

Sosa handed the men the briefcases and they took him to his mom's mansion in a remote area.

***

ACROSS TOWN

Ashley saw her men arrive with Sosa, but she really was looking for the money in tow. When seeing the two briefcases, she put her gun down and smiled opening the front door for her son.

"Hey, my handsome son." She hugged him as if this was the first time in years they laid eyes on each other.

"What's going on?" Sosa walked inside the polished place.

"How was the flight?" Ashley asked while her men followed them into the living room

"Long but comfortable."

"Y'all go count the money and let me know if a dollar is missing," Ashley told her goons with a smile right in front of Sosa.

"Damn, you don't trust me?"

"I don't trust nobody but how's business in Philly?" She sat down eating fruit off a tray.

"Same shit but I just got the Feds and DEA on my ass."

"You need help?"

"Nah, I believe I can handle it," he replied.

"You positive because I know some very powerful people." She suggested.

"I'm okay. I like to send messages," Sosa stated.

"The product should be in your city tomorrow night. I sent it to Bless."

"Aight. I like how he be getting it through."

"Well, listen make yourself at home. I'ma go food shopping so I can cook for you." Ashley got up to leave as Sosa took a cat nap.

CHAPTER 36
DOWNTOWN PHILLY

The chief of police of the FBI, Mr. Sims stopped his paperwork to text his side bitch so they could meet up before he went home to his wife and kids. Mr. Sims was a successful black man in his late forties with a beautiful wife and children by her, but he loved to have a little fun. His wife didn't do certain things that his mistress did like suck dick nasty, take it in her ass, or she didn't eat his butthole, which was not the best feeling he experienced.

Normally, he was the last one in the office so tonight wasn't so different as he wrapped things up to leave. Working on the Sosa Gang case and the Outlaws case had to be harder than when he did the Junior Mafia case out of Philly a few decades ago.

Another text came in with an addy to a hotel his mistress was at waiting on him nice and wet. Mr. Sims rushed out his office as he was horny and careless. While speed walking outside a call came in from his wife.

"Fuck …" he said knowing he had to answer, or she would go crazy on him and bleach his clothes.

"Hey honey," he answered, putting her on speaker.

"What you doing?"

"At work." He lied to his wife as he always did, and it came out naturally.

"What time you coming home tonight?" She asked him

"I got a few more reports to do and then I'm on my way baby. I promise." He lied so smooth.

"Okay, I love you."

"Love you too. Kiss the kids goodnight for me." Mr. Sims went as hard as blowing a kiss into the phone.

Mr. Sims laughed to himself as he went to Germantown, which is the location she gave him.

He liked young dancers who worked in clubs and who knew how to keep their mouths closed.

The twenty minute ride was short as he thought about all the positions he wanted to put his mistress in. She was flexible.

Once he arrived at the hotel, he read the text again to get the room number and it was 302 on the upper level.

Mr. Sims rocked a daddy's hat, trying to be low key because he couldn't afford to jeopardize his family or the career he dreamed of having since a little kid.

The door room was open like always as he slid inside, hearing the shower running and wanting to surprise her. Mr. Sims got naked and crept into the bathroom, hoping to fuck her slim ass in the shower.

He walked closer to the shower and quickly pulled the curtains back to see nobody.

"What the fuck?" He says turning off the water.

When Mr. Sims turned around, he saw Lil Hak pointing a gun in his face and smiling.

Come out here, dummy. You was so thirsty. You ain't pay no attention to the dead bitch under the bed," Lil Hak says dragging him by his collar out into the bed area.

"I'ma a fucking agent!" Mr. Sims yelled only to hear Lil Hak laugh at his comment. He saw his mistress' whole arm and hair sticking out from under the hotel room bed.

"I don't give a fuck, old head. You put yourself in a bad situation."

"The government don't have enough to railroad you. I been trying to find shit but it's hard. Y'all smart but Agent Limb and Maura may have shit to get you all arrested." He tried to clear himself out the way, but Lil Hak didn't buy it.

"Thank you anyway, bull but this ain't on me, old head." Lil Hak pulled the trigger twice, killing him and leaving. Lil Jet was parked outside.

Lil Hak thought about what the agent said about the other two cops. He would sure tell Sosa whenever he came back from Colombia.

Every time Sosa came back from Colombia, he would flood them with coke. Lil Hak was about to purchase a house and a Rolls Royce this week.

Getting into the car, he heard Lil Jet singing an old Cassidy song.

"Damn young bull, you still fucking with the old head?" Lil Hak asked climbing in the passenger seat.

"Hell yeah, he used to be my favorite rapper."

"Me too, but he washed up now. What's up with Beth? She saved Twin ass a few weeks ago I heard," says Lil Hak.

'She pregnant, bro. We just getting back on track." Lil Jet knew Beth was a handful, but she was loyal and a real bitch.

"Yeah, bro, keep her. She rare."

"Facts. I'ma drop you off and go home now," Lil Jet said.

"Aight bet."

Romell Tukes

CHAPTER 37
DARBY, PHILLY

Lil Jet pulled up to his crib after a long night outside fucking with Lil Hak, who was a fucking maniac.

He knew Beth was sleep because she'd been doing a lot of that lately. Every pregnant woman liked to get a lot of sleep and eat things they craved.

Beth loved being pregnant again and it brought their relationship closer, much closer. Shit was getting bad between them since Lil Jet got shot by Dirty. That's when she started to find texts in his phone from other women and shit went left.

Lil Jet slipped up and confessed to it, asking for her forgiveness so they could move on.

Being there with her throughout Beth's new pregnancy meant a lot. It showed her how much Lil Jet really cared.

He walked into the house and into to his bedroom. When he opened the room door, Beth was up, to his surprise, reading a hood novel called Life of a Savage by an Author named Romell Tukes.

"Hey sexy," Lil Jet said seeing Beth in a gown looking cute.

"Come lay down," she eagerly said as he did as she said.

"You miss me, huh?"

"I'ma show you how much I miss you, daddy." Beth went below the covers until she got to his cock. She wrapped her lips around his penis as Lil Jet tangled his fingers in her hair. She dragged her mouth up and down the rod.

"Hmmmm …" he moaned, loving the way she sucked dick. On her way up, she paused at the top to suck his tip as he trusted his hips into her face.

Beth flicked her tongue in the tiny slit while she cradled his balls. She was deep throating his length, taking him all the way down her throat.

Ready for dick, she climbed onto his pole. She straddled his waist while grasping the base of his dick and guided it into Beth's super wetness.

"Ohhh yessss baby ..." she moaned out loud, going down inch by inch on his rod.

Lil Jet fucked her for a few more hours before they held each other and talked for a while before going to sleep.

***

MIAMI, FL

Foxy and Rizzy recently got off of the flight about forty minutes ago and now they were about to have the time of their life. Rizzy just purchased a Rolls Royce down from Exotic Rentals, something they can stunt in because almost every car the couple saw was foreign.

"Baby, we should move out here one day," says Foxy.

"Out to Miami?" Rizzy said, driving to their hotel.

"Yeah."

"Okay, let's get a condo out here," Rizzy stated.

"Today?" She got hyped.

"Yeah, we about to go crib shopping right now. Let's slide to see what they have in North Miami," he said as they stopped at a red light.

Rizzy punched in condos for sale in the iPhone search system.

"I got a question and I want you to be honest," she looked him in his eyes, holding his hand.

"What's up?"

"Do you see yourself spending the rest of your life with me?" She asked a question that had been on her mind.

"Yes."

"You said that real fast," she joked not knowing if Rizzy was serious or just fucking around.

"I really love you, Foxy because we are similar in a lot of ways and also opposites. Our connection is on a different level," he told her while driving down South Beach to see beautiful women all over the place in tiny bikinis.

"You know what to say, don't you?" She smiled as Rizzy always made her feel good and loved unlike any other man in her life.

164

"You want kids?" Rizzy asked because he wanted a few.

"Yes."

"How many?"

"A football team." She laughed but very serious. Since a little girl, Foxy wanted her own family.

"I can make that happen."

"I bet you can, but the question is will you help me take care of them?" She knew how most niggas were.

"One thing about me, I take care of mine." He confirmed.

"Is that right?"

"Facts."

"Well, maybe I should get off my birth control soon," she stated.

"If that's what you want to do, then I'm all for it, baby."

"Okay, cool," Foxy stated smiling, hoping he was ready for what comes with a long-term relationship.

Romell Tukes

CHAPTER 38
DOWNTOWN PHILLY
FBI BUILDING

Elina heard there was someone else taking her boss' spot since he got killed in a hotel with a hooker. That was the word going around in the building. The rumor was a pimp killed her boss and the hooker, but Elina knew better. There has to be more to the story.

Sosa texted her letting Elina know he got back in town and he would be stopping by later. There bond spoke for itself but she wanted more sexually. Not tonight because her period just came on and running red lights wasn't her thing at all.

"Maura, the new boss wants to see you and warning, he is a fucking dickhead. You wouldn't believe what he told me," Agent Limb said approaching her desk.

"I can only imagine." She joked.

"He tells me I got one time to fuck up on anything and he would fire my white ass because he don't like no white people," Agent Limb said never meeting a man like the new rude boss.

"Sounds like a good boss to me." She laughed, getting up to meet the new chief of the FBI.

Elina knocked on the glass window and a black man with a gray beard on the phone waved her to come inside. Walking in the office full of African statues, she could tell he was into the culture.

She listened to his conversation on the phone as he went in on whoever he spoke out.

"I don't give a fuck who you are, Dick. I want this done in a week notice," Her new boss says rudely before he hung up on the caller.

Elina saw the name on the desk that read Bomzaboa, which had to be an African man and not to mention, he was black as shit.

"Agent Maura, you have a very impressive record in the FBI unlike anything I've saw in a long time," He said reading her file the same way he did all the agents but none of them caught his attention. Except her.

"Thank you."

"As you know, someone killed your boss, so I'll be the new head nigga in charge," he told her.

"Good to know."

"We need more black people in this building. Soon, I'll be doing a lot of firing and hiring. We need Spanish and blacks in here," he stated.

"I agree."

"Hope so, but before you go, I'm letting you know this just because I like you. Normally, I wouldn't tell nobody shit because I'm the boss."

"Okay." Elina had no idea what he was talking about.

"The case against the Outlaws and the Sosa Gang are dropped," he said relaxed.

"What ... how?"

"It's too many loopholes that will have us looking bad in court," he told her, making sense and she knew this.

Elina thought for a second, this could be good news for Sosa. She couldn't wait to tell him tonight.

"Aight. I guess if you feel like this is the right choice, I'm all aboard with you." She got up to leave.

"I'm not done yet. Now that I'm dropping those cases, I'm opening up a case on Sosa and Vera. They are now our targets. Have a good day Elina or Agent Maura," he told Elina calling her by both names only few knew about.

Elina walked out his office feeling there was something very bad about to happen and deep down, she knew her name was about to be all up in shit.

***

FORT WASHINGTON, PHILLY

Sosa liked Elina's crib as he walked up the stairs to the front door of the brick house in the middle of a quiet middle class neighborhood.

At first, he wasn't going to come because he knew deep down, she could have ill intentions just like Allure did. Elina'd been saving his ass for a while now and he took that for what it was worth. The door flew open, and he saw Elina looking cute in a short pink dress with heels on showing her cute feet.

"Hey." She gave him a hug, but her energy wasn't where it normally was. He peeped it walking in too.

"You okay?" Sosa smelled some good food cooking while admiring the inside of the nice size house.

"I'm not to be honest, Sosa because I have a new boss and he dismissed the Sosa Gang and Outlaw cases."

"Oh, shit that's good." He couldn't believe it.

"Yes, but he's starting a case on you and Vera." Elina saw his face drop.

"Fuck. Why the hell he want me?" Sosa sat down thinking that killing her last boss was going get rid of the problem but now it seemed as if he had a bigger one.

"I'ma find out but I don't know his agenda. Something isn't right with him."

"Don't worry. Let's eat and watch a movie," Sosa said as they did just that. That night, they fell asleep in each other's arms.

Romell Tukes

CHAPTER 39
MIAMI, FL

Foxy and Rizzy spent their last day in Miami jet skiing having a blast on South Beach where they rented out the jet skis for a hundred dollars an hour so they could have a good time.

Miami had been a blast for the last week as they went to clubs, diners, shopping on Collins Ave, and enjoying everything Miami had to offer them.

Staying at the Blue Fountain Hotel had so much shit to do inside that they never really had to leave. The trip made them closer and really appreciate each other more. They both saw a lot of beautiful men and women in the city, but their eyes been glued to each other since arriving.

Rizzy did tricks on the jet skis in the water as Foxy tried to keep up but couldn't because she was scared of falling into the clear water.

Seeing Foxy so far behind, he slowed down, letting her catch up as Rizzy stopped in the middle of the ocean.

"You can't keep up, babe?" Rizzy said, seeing Foxy's hair soaked looking sexy.

"Hell no. I'm not speeding through the ocean to fall in with the sharks. Nigga you wilding the fuck out," she said patting down her edges.

"This was your idea."

"I thought we was going to ride on the jet skis together," she responded.

"You got to learn to face your fears in life, baby."

"I don't fear nothing except Allah," she stated.

"How about we do some nasty shit right here?" She said, looking around to see a few jet skis speeding on the water.

"What you want to do?" He said, climbing onto her jet ski getting behind her.

Rizzy pulled out his dick and slid her bikini to the side and entered her tight pussy.

"Uhmmmm …" She moaned, backing up on his cock and holding the handlebars as she soaked on to his cock. He grabbed her waist as she grinded up and down on his pole going crazy making a quick fast fuck in the middle of the water.

Other people saw this, but they minded their own business, knowing sex on the beach or in the water was regular in the 305.

***

TEMPLE UNIVERSITY, PHILLY

Zarhya had a late-night class which started at 7 PM and she was just now coming from work. Things had been super busy. She didn't even have a chance to enjoy the summer, which was almost over. In two weeks, her birthday would be here and Zarhya really wanted to go out to Vegas with her girls but not only was she backed up in school, she was low on funds. She knew Sosa would hit her off with some money but deep down, it would not feel right because it wasn't clean money. Not one to knock nobody's hustle but she rather not be a part of something she knew was wrong

The car her mom got Zarhya, she sold last month because she didn't even want to look at it after the way her mom abandoned her and the family when they was growing up.

Pulling into parking lot C, a call from Sosa appeared so she placed the call on speaker.

"Long time no speak, bro," she answered not seeing or hearing from him since her birthday.

"I'm sorry."

"For what?"

"Not reaching out, sis. Things been real shaky around here." Sosa tried to tell her in so many words that shit was really looking bad in Philly for the street life.

"Maybe you need a new career or lifestyle." She added while parking

"Shit, I went legit but that shit ain't got me nowhere," Sosa stated.

"You gotta have patience, Sean."

"Patience in a man is hard to practice, sis. Especially, when a person is used to a certain way of living," he told her.

"There is nothing that you can't change," Zarhya told him.

"I'ma go to this class. I will call you when I get out," Zarhya says, getting out the car to see a car pull up behind her.

"Okay, I love you," he said.

"Love you too, bro. Be safe and smart," she told him before hanging up

When Zarhya got out of the car, a pretty Hispanic woman approached her.

"Excuse me, but can you help me get a certain dorm to find my niece?" The woman asked.

"What dorm is your niece in? I'm in a little rush," Zarhya says as the woman went into her purse for a piece of paper.

The woman pulled out a gun and aimed it at Zarhya, who mouth dropped.

Bloc, Bloc, Bloc, Bloc, Bloc, Bloc, Bloc ...

Vera shot Zaryha in her face, neck ,and chest before walking off.

Romell Tukes

CHAPTER 40
DOWNTOWN PHILLY

Janasia had been going hard at work, day and night trying to cover Lez's tracks and put the light on Sosa Gang and take it off of her crew.

With her boss dead, his position was open, and nobody had filled it yet. The big boss was said to come down today.

"Hey Janasia," a man named Ryle said walking into her office.

"Ryle, how's the wife and kids?" She asked knowing how Ryle always tried to flirt with her on the daily.

"They're fine, have you heard anything about Thornton's death?" He asked.

"No, have you?"

"Not yet but I personally think it could have been one of them hoodlum crews that we need to get off the streets," says Ryle leaning on the wall.

"I think it could have been them guys from the Badlands." She threw out there to fish.

"You locked all of them up, didn't you?"

"There are still some out there that I need to get." She confirmed.

"Oh well, we need to get them fuckers off the streets," he told her, seeing a group of people enter the building.

"That's them?" Janasia said looking out her window.

"Yeah, that's the boss, Mr. Madison," says Ryle leaving her office so he could go suck dick for a promotion. Janasia stopped worked and took a deep breath before getting up to watch all her co-workers suck cock for a position, mainly Thornton's spot. She stood in the middle of the office for five minutes, hearing the big boss call her name which confused her.

"Me?" she pointed at herself.

"Yes, you're Janasia, right?" Mr. Madison, a tall white man stated walking up to her all smiles.

"Yes I am."

"I've seen a lot of your work and I'm overly impressed by your work ethic," Mr. Madison told her.

"Thanks, I'm just doing my job." She shot back, playing the humble role.

"Would you like a promotion because I need someone to fill the late Mr. Thornton's spot?" Mr. Madison stated.

"Hold on, you want me to be the boss?"

"Yes, if you're willing?" He spoke.

"Of course."

"Great. Congratulations on your new promotion. You will be hearing from me soon." Mr. Madison walked off, leaving the building.

"What happened? He fired you?" Ryle quizzed.

"No, actually, I'm your boss now," she said, smiling.

"No fucking way." He couldn't believe it a female was about to run the show.

"Yep, I'm about to change this whole place." She walked off smiling and laughing as her co-workers gossiped about her.

**

SOUTHWEST, PHILLY

Sosa came out to the projects to chill with Lil Hak, who was surrounded by the gang and doing everything legal outside. He was not giving a fuck.

Last night, Sosa got a call from one of Zarhya's friends saying she was shot dead on the college campus.

At first he didn't want to believe it until he hung up the phone and saw the breaking news. Zarhya's picture flashed across the screen stating how she was killed and how good of a student she was in school. He needed to come out and get sum air today, losing his only sister hit him hard.

"You straight, young bull." Lil Hak sat next to him, passing Sosa a bottle of Henny.

"I ain't got no choice but to be aight cuz someone took my sister, bro. On some real nigga shit bull, I feel like life always gives me the shit end of almost every situation. From the good to the bad." Sosa admitted sadly.

"Don't let this tear you down, cuz. I know your strength as a man. You damn near carried a whole city on your back, cuz. Facts," says Lil Hak hating to see his boy down bad like this.

"Facts. I'ma just make it right, cuz. I can't cry over it. The only way I'ma feel better is if I kill whoever did this."

"You got a clue?"

"Not really but there are only but so many people who would even have the balls to do this," Sosa said thinking while he drank Henny out of the bottle.

"Lez?"

"Nah, he wouldn't do that. Lez would just gun for us." Sosa added.

"I ain't heard from Foxy and Rizzy lately." Lil Hak knew Foxy was up to no good.

"Fuck them bro but I think I may have a person in mind." Sosa thought about Allure who knew Zarhya went to Temple, and they even had a cool little bond.

Romell Tukes

CHAPTER 41
YEADON, PHILLY

Vera and Allure both was chilling in their new home, decorating it, and making it cozy.

"I should go get some curtains I saw at this new designer store," Vera said, walking into the dining room where Allure was eating.

"What store, mom?" Allure'd been home for a few days. She wanted to spend some time with Vera for her mom's up and coming birthday.

"In downtown Philly next to the City Center."

"I'll go because I want to get some things from the liquor store," Allure got up and grabbed her purse and phone.

"You sure, baby? I know you just got back from your trip," says Vera who was ready to slide.

"I want to get something from the store anyway. I'm on my period so I need some tampons," Allure said leaving needing to get some fresh air anyway.

"Okay, use my car." Vera gave Allure the keys to her Benz.

"Do you need anything?"

"No baby. I'ma start cooking." Vera went into the kitchen.

Allure left, thinking about what Sosa was doing and if he had a new girlfriend now or was he thinking about the same way she did. Even though Allure chose her mom's side and had a shootout with Sosa, she still loved him. Every night, he was on her brain, and she wished he would hear things from her point of view. At times, she hoped one day he would forgive her and accept the person she was, even with Vera and his beef. Allure felt like she chose the wrong side because deep down she understood the love her mom had for her, but the love Sosa gave to Allure was unconditional.

The ride to the shopping center was nearby so she got there quickly and entered the liquor store first to get a few bottles of Henny and Patron. She found herself drinking a lot lately to wash away the pain and hurt Sosa was putting her through.

"Excuse me, where is the D'usse?" Allure asked one of the store workers.

"In the back next to the Moet. It's behind the counter," The man said putting bottles on the shelves.

"Thank you," Allure says, catching the man looking at her ass.

Once getting the D'usse, she left the store about to pick up them curtains for her mom. Allure placed the bags in her backseat and that's when she felt the bullet hit her lower back.

Bloc, Bloc, Bloc ...

Allure was caught off guard. Her body turned around soaking into her car. She was looking at Sosa stand over her in all black.

"Why you had to go against me? I really loved you," Sosa said from his heart.

"I love you," she said, taking her last breath and gasping for air.

"Too late."

Bloc, Bloc ...

Sosa put two more bullets in her skull, finishing what he started as he smoothly walked off into the dark parking lot.

He'd been following her since she got back into the city, and it was now or never. Killing the woman he loved took a lot out of him. If he ain't do it then, he knew she would have got him out the way.

***

FDC, PHILLY

Barry waited inside the room used for a lawyer visit. He couldn't sit still as he waited for his lawyer. Prison was starting to fuck with his head. The stress, his case, the time, the people and losing family members did it to him. When he got the news about his daughter's death, he felt like soul was already dead and left his body. Zarhya was his baby girl. He couldn't believe she got killed at her college and he knew who did it. He blamed Sosa. Barry felt like this was his son's fault because he was supposed to be watching over her.

His lawyer, Mr. Fairly came in with a woman he never saw but she was very beautiful.

"Barry," his lawyer said having a seat to get this meeting started.

"Who is this?"

"This is the head of the DEA, Ms. Janasia. Tell her what you told me over the phone because she will be handling that case," Mr. Fairly said as Janasia gave Barry a smile.

"Nice to meet you, Barry. Don't feel discouraged from doing the right thing. I'm sure this will be a big help to your own case," Janasia said.

"Who the fuck are you?" Barry didn't feel comfortable talking in front of Janasia because he ain't know her from a can of paint.

"I'm the bitch that's gonna get you a time cut, or your cases dropped. It's on you to play little girl games or do what's right for yourself," she told him seeing he wasn't trying to hear it. Barry called his lawyer and told him he had info that could get him out.

"Barry, you need Janasia. Without her help, you're stuck and there is nothing that will help as of now. Not even a fucking miracle." His lawyer got real with him knowing Barry was fucked without Vaseline.

"Aight, but how much can she help me?" Barry asked.

"It depends?" She replied ready to take notes and pulling out a pen and a yellow pad.

"On what?" Barry asked back, hoping she wasn't about to play no games.

"How valid is your story?" Mr. Fairly answered for her.

"I'ma tell you how this work. Barry, you gonna tell me everything and I'ma go look into it," she told Barry who looked like he wanted to get up and leave out of the room.

"You okay with that Barry?" Mr. Fairly asked.

"What choice do I have?" Barry replied.

"Janasia is very trustworthy and a woman of her word," Mr. Fairly says, trying to stamp Janasia.

"Okay, the person I'm about to give y'all is one of the biggest suppliers in Philly," says Barry.

"I need names." She added.

"My son, Sosa," Barry said with no type of shame or remorse.

"You snitching on your own son?" She asked, somewhat used to people giving up their loved ones.

"He not my son no more."

"You just said he was." Mr. Fairly added.

"Do you want the information or what?" Barry got upset because he already felt low for ratting, but they was making him feel worse.

"Question, why him?" Janasia asked.

"Because I created a monster and if I don't get him off the street, more people will die but he's not the only one I got to give," Barry said.

"Oh no?" Janasia wrote down every word.

"The Outlaws. I know one of their leaders. His name is Imam Ahmad, but they have other members. I will find out their names soon," Barry said, seeing Janasia get very uncomfortable.

"I've heard of them," Mr. Fairly said in deep thought.

"Tell me more," Janasia said knowing Barry was about to be a big problem because Imam Ahmad could easily link back to her.

"Sosa killed my son, Block and a few more people. I'll write down the days and locations," Barry admitted.

"Will you be willing to stand at trial and take an oath on all of this?" Janasia asked.

"Yep." Barry shot back quick

"Okay, tell me everything from the start." Janasia was at the jail for hours taking notes.

CHAPTER 42
UPTOWN, PHILLY

Dirty was in a courthouse trying to pay some backed up tickets which came up to a thousand dollars in all and if he ain't pay it today, they would try to tow his Audi.

Shit had been a little calm or things was waiting to blow up any minute. Dirty hated when shit got quiet, and niggas were MIA because that meant niggas were plotting in his mind.

Vera recently dropped him off some more product to hold Dirty and Lez over while she buried her daughter. Neither one of the men knew she even had a daughter because Vera kept her life private.

"I'm trying pay for my tickets." Dirty asked the stank looking white woman sitting at a desk behind a window.

"ID, please?"

"Here you go." Dirty handed her his ID while she punched numbers into the computer system.

"You have a thousand dollars backed up in fines." She looked up from her computer at him, knowing how black people was always late at paying shit. She wasn't surprised.

"I know that's why I'm here," says Dirty, pulling out a wad of money to give her.

"Okay, I'll clear them up for you now," she said knowing it had to be drug money because he looked like a dope dealer. Just like the rest of them.

Dirty got his tickets cleared and walked out the courthouse, seeing his little bro called him from Northeast. He was most likely waiting on his order. About to dial the number, he just so happened to look up and saw Lil Jet creeping across the street with a Draco to his side.

Dirty was naked with no gun and when he turned around, he saw the old white lady who helped him clear his tickets going on her lunch break.

Tat, Tat, Tat, Tat, Tat, Tat, Tat, Tat, Tat, Tat, Tat …

Dirty grabbed the white woman and used her as a shield while making his way back into the building. The woman's body was rattled with bullets as Lil Jet tried to gun Dirty down for almost taking his life months ago.

Tat, Tat, Tat, Tat, Tat, Tat, Tat,

Bullets hit the courthouse and two guards saw Dirty running in the building as the white woman's body was slumped in the doorway.

Lil Jet saw Dirty got away and ran up the block where Twin was parked.

They followed Dirty to the courthouse since they caught him leaving IHOP this morning. Twin thought it was a bad idea to have a shootout in broad daylight in front of a courthouse.

"You hit him bro?" Twin said when Lil Jet got inside looking frustrated.

"Nah."

"Next time. Don't trip, cuz."

Twin pulled off knowing Dirty would pop up again sooner than later.

"Let's go to the funeral." Lil Jet referred to Zarhya's funeral.

***

Southwest, Philly
Meanwhile

Zarhya's funeral was held outside today. On this nice day, there had to be at least two hundred and fifty people there to pay respect to the beautiful young woman. Sosa sat in the front row next to his mom and his uncle Bless as a black pastor led the ceremony.

"You need to find out who did this and meet me at the hotel. I won't watch my daughter get put in the ground," Ashley said, getting up to leave with four men in suits who were her security.

"I will," he said, not really in the mood to talk.

Twin and Lil Jet pulled up parking behind the row of cars parked in the long line on the pathway.

"Who the fuck is that?" Lil Jet said seeing Ashley and her goons hopping in a Rolls Royce limousine with tints.

"I have no fucking clue." Twin walked onto the grass and posted up next to a group of Sosa Gang members who came with Lil Hak.

"Where y'all been at?" Lil Hak stated to Lil Jet and Twin seeing they arrived late to the funeral because they all came out to show Sosa support.

Losing a family member felt like taking something big from each of their hearts. When one of them lost a family member, they all felt that pain.

"We saw Dirty on the way here," Lil Jet stated, still upset that he missed his target a few minutes ago.

"Y'all got his bitch ass?' Lil Hak got hyped knowing they killed their number one enemy right now.

"Nah nigga, why don't you go put in same work?" Lil Jet said walking off.

"He in his bag," says Lil Hak

"Facts, though. He'll be okay," Twin stated as the funeral was close to being over.

Romell Tukes

CHAPTER 43
DOWNTOWN, PHILLY

Ashley stayed at one of the nicest hotels in the city just for a few days until she headed back home to Colombia. Her daughter's death took a lot out of Ashley to the point where she couldn't even look at Zarhya in the casket. The guilty conscious kicked in when she made it to the funeral. Not having a solid or any foundation with her daughter made her feel like shit and now it was something Ashley would have to live with until death.

Bless was in the bathroom and Sosa should be there any minute. She asked him to come by to speak with her about business arrangements.

The knock made her get up and answer the door as she took the glass of red wine with her.

"What's good, you straight?" Sosa asked walking inside the nice hotel.

"Yeah, I have no choice, baby," she told him.

"I think you should have stayed at the funeral, mom," he told her.

"I can't watch my child get buried. Especially someone so innocent, Sean. We're gangsters by blood. Your sister didn't deserve to get murdered," she said as Bless came out of the bathroom from taking a long shit.

"I understand," Sosa confirmed.

"Nephew, what's up?" Bless said sitting down and reaching for a bottle of liquor to drink.

"Same shit, bro. Y'all about to head out?" Asked Sosa.

"Yeah, I'm just waiting for your mom so we can bounce to the West," says Bless pulling out some Cali weed he wanted to roll up.

"Before we go I want to have a little meeting with you both," Ashley said calmly, happy to have her family around.

"What's wrong, mom?"

"We have a problem. Someone we deal with is going behind our backs making deals with the enemy trying to snake us out of our spot," Ashley said with her head down.

"I bet you it's that nigga, Rico," Bless stated knowing Rico couldn't be trusted at all.

"Damn, this shit don't stop," Sosa said not understanding the grimy part of how this game go.

"The problem is the snake is in our own circle," says Ashley looking at Sosa, pulling out a gun and aiming at her son.

"I knew this fool was playing us!" Bless shouted, looking at Sosa jumping up and pumped up.

"I'm sorry love," Ashley says, turning the gun on Bless.

Boc, Boc, Boc, Boc, Boc, Boc, Boc …

Bless' body fell into the couch, holding his chest as bullets pierced heart and organs. The bullets killed him instantly.

Sosa took a deep breath. He thought it was over, but he wasn't about to beg for his life.

"Sean, your uncle been making side moves with other families and dipping in the pack. He was about to have both of us killed tonight. His men were on their way up here but now they all work for me," Ashley said.

"Wow, how you find out?"

"I have my ways, son." She smiled

"Guess you can't trust nobody in the game."

"Nobody, not even me. Now, go home. I'll get with you in the morning," she tells him, taking a seat next to her brother's dead body. She placed an arm around him to talk with the dead man, drinking her wine.

Sosa left knowing his mom was still suffering from mental health problems seeing this with his own eyes. He always felt there was something off about Bless, but he didn't look too far into it. Everything been happening so fast. His sister's death, Allure's death, Bless' death and the drama but Sosa knew this is the life he signed up for.

**

FORT WASHINGTON PHILLY

"What the fuck, Sean." Elina collapsed on her queen size bed drained from the rough, crazy sex Sosa just put on her ass.

Sosa needed a relief, so he called Elina who was waiting for him at her door, ass naked. Last time he was over there, they just watched TV and chilled, but Elina made sure she got her some dick this time.

The other day he told her about the death of his sister and Elina couldn't believe it because Zarhya was a good girl. They were very close. Elina used to take Zarhya out every weekend to shop or get her hair and nails done up when she was with Barry during her undercover investigation.

"You good, Sean?"

"Yeah, I'ma be okay. I just gotta focus up, mami."

"Don't let Zarhya's death make you go backwards."

"I'm not."

"You know who did it?"

"Not yet." Sosa lied already on Vera's ass.

"You don't need him. I can do some work and look into it," she asked, twirling her nails on his chest.

"I'll be fine, but thanks."

'Oh, I forgot to tell you that one of my coworkers got word Barry is about to start working with the government. I never thought I would see this day," Elina said as Sosa raised up.

"My dad, Barry. Are you sure?"

"Hell yeah. They said he got some shit going on with the DEA."

"Fuck, this is crazy." Sosa got out of her bed thinking all the shit his dad knew about him.

"Everything will be fine, Sean. He have to prove whatever he says, and I know your smart enough to cover your tracks," she says.

"I gotta go."

"When are you coming back?" She asked, already missing his dick.

"Soon." Sosa got dressed and left trying to clear his mind.

Romell Tukes

CHAPTER 44
FDC, PHILLY

Barry just came back to his cell from breakfast to see his celly sitting at the desk reading the noble Quran as he did early in the morning every day.

"As-salaam-alaikum," Barry greeted his celly, Yaqeen, who was a young man from South Philly just sentenced to seventy-six years in the feds.

"Walaikum-Salaam, brother. What they had for breakfast?" asked Yaqeen, which meant certainty in Islam.

"The same thing Bran Flakes, milk, apple sauce, and a muffin."

"Oh nah, I'm straight on that shit. I'm about to go exercise real quick," Yaqeen says walking out the small cell they had to share with a bunk, toilet, and small desk.

"I'ma use the bathroom and hop on the computer," Barry said, putting the curtain up which was tissue he stuck on the window frame so people wouldn't look in his cell.

Once he was safe, Barry pulled out a cell phone from his mattress and hit the redial button.

"This is Janasia speaking."

"I got more news. My celly, Yaqeen told me about two murders he committed two years ago when he was free." said Barry in a low pitch voice so nobody outside his cell could hear him. Even if they did, he would play crazy and say he be talking to his self.

"Where did the crimes happen, Barry. I need location and days," Janasia said on the other end.

"I'll try tonight."

"Okay, you're doing a good job. Top Flight Security shit." She joked.

"I'm just trying get free."

"Free your mind. You will be okay." She assured him "For now, that will have to do but trust me, Barry, your time will come soon," she told him before hanging up.

Barry flushed the toilet acting like he was taking a shit then hidden his flip phone under his mattress.

Since ratting on his son, Sosa, and Imam Ahmad, he took it upon himself to build cases on niggas in jail to help him get brownie points with the DEA.

Barry walked out of his cell to use the computer so he could see if any messages came in today.

The thing about the feds was inmates could use Corrlink emails and telephones to contact their loved ones.

Getting on the computer, he saw there were three new messages in blue bold letters. When he clicked on the box to open his emails, the unit got quiet. Before he looked there was movement behind him as if someone was running behind Barry. Yaqeen stabbed him with a long sharp blade in his neck and the head four times. He pushed him on the floor and started to work his knife into Barry's heart and chest. Correctional officers rushed the unit three minutes later by that time Barry was already in a puddle of blood dead.

Yaqeen laid on the floor with a knife tied to a shoelace surrendering as they cuffed him up while looking down the unit for a murder scene. The whole dorm was in shock to see the crime scene take place in the middle of the dayroom like that.

Yaqeen was an Outlaw member so when he got word that Barry had to be killed and there was one on his head he felt it was only right to look out for his gang since he wouldn't see light or day again anyway.

Janasia knew Barry would be a big problem if she didn't handle it correctly. Not only was Imam Ahmad connected to her, but it could fuck up all her plans.

Barry telling on Sosa didn't hold too much weight because he was already hot on the law enforcement radars.

Yaqeen went to the box with a big smile on his face knowing he would have looked at the account within the next hour. He knew Barry's morning routine every morning, so he carefully plotted the scene out for a few now and was pleased with the results.

York, PA

Imam Ahmad and Vera been chilling at one of her properties she owned. They been fucking and sucking each other for two days straight both getting off their stress.

Vera was still torn over Allure's death and Imam Ahmad was worried about his safety from Twin.

"You need a trip somewhere out the country," Imam Ahmad told her.

"Maybe when this is all over. I've lost my sister, brother, and now my daughter to some kids I've just recently heard of." Vera walked into the kitchen to get her bottle of wine so she could drink. Something she's been doing a lot of these days.

"I got a plan," Imam Ahmad said, hoping' she would be down.

"What?"

"I can't really tell you now, but I just need to know if your down?"

"Yes."

"Give me a week." Imam Ahmad got up and left her crib to put his plan together.

Romell Tukes

CHAPTER 45
DOWNTOWN, PHILLY

Elina couldn't believe what hit her desk this morning. It was a ghostly and horrifying photo of Barry with stab marks all over his face and upper body. Barry didn't even look recognizable from the photo, reading the recapitulation of the incident report. It read an Outlaw member stabbed Barry because he skipped him in line. She reminisced about recently telling Sosa how his dad was telling but now, Elina wonders if Sosa had anything to do with this because he had a recalcitrant and stubborn way of taking information.

Elina stepped out of the office, nodding at a few agents as she walked into the staircase to call Sosa. Sosa picked up on the third ring.

"Ayo."

"Hey, it's me, Elina."

"Hi sexy, what's going on?" He replied driving with Lil Hak to handle some business. Sosa already informed his crew what the deal was between him and Elina.

"Something bad happened."

"Huh?"

"I said something happened. Can you hear me?" Elina repeated hearing his phone was going in and outta service.

"What are you talking about?" Sosa could tell by her voice something was wrong on the phone.

"Your father was stabbed to death in prison yesterday by an Outlaw member," she told him.

"I don't have a father."

"Well Barry," she corrected herself, sensing he didn't really give a shit.

"I'm sure he'll be okay."

"Sean, he's gone."

"Good for him but I'ma hit you back tonight. I'm driving," he said.

"Be safe." She hung up right on time as a few officers came out to go on their lunch break.

"Maura," two of them said, walking past her giving off a fake smile. Everybody at the job was full of shit. Elina really hated it but luckily, she saw the bigger picture.

***

NORTHEAST, PHILLY

Twin walked through the long hallway of the nursing home which smelled like shitty diapers. His grandmom birthday was today so he came by to give her same flowers and be there.

Growing up, his grandmom on his mom side played a big role in how he grew up. When she got old two years ago, he placed her in the best nursing home in the city.

He saw her door was open as he walked inside to see his grandmom, Mrs. Federer threading a blanket.

"Hey, grandmom," Twin said as she looked up and smiled.

Twin could tell there was no progress with his grandmom health and mental. She still didn't know who he was or where she was at.

Handing her the flowers, he heard a crack in the wood floor, turning around. Imam Ahmad posted up right behind him with a gun to his face.

"I knew you would be here today, my son." Imam Ahmad wore an all-black garment with a gold strip.

"All this because I ain't want to join your lame ass crew?" Twin said as he saw his grandma watch as if it was a TV show.

"No, all of this because you disobeyed me as your father."

"Maybe if you was a real father, I would have," Twin replied with a blank look on his face.

"I did the best I could as a man for our brother. May his soul rest in peace and Traina, my baby girl that your people took from me."

"Your crew took Traina," Twin corrected his father.

"It didn't matter now. She gone and so are you bitch ..."

BOOM ... BOOM ... BOOM ...BOOM ...

196

Twin body hit the floor as Mrs. Federer had a shocked look on her face before Imam Ahmad shot her twice in the chest, making the frail lady fall out of the chair.

"I never liked you anyway," Imam Ahmad said, rushing out through the back to meet up with Vera, who was waiting on him. Imam Ahmad had to get Twin out the way so he could now break in Sosa's circle and takes over his castle very shortly. The plans he wanted to achieve would take a lot of time and a few people he was gonna need on his new team, but all the dead weight needed to be eliminated.

"That was fast baby," Vera said as he got in the truck.

"It's finished."

"You did good."

"I'ma call a meeting with everybody so we can all get on the same page. I got a feeling Sosa gonna be easier to kill if this works."

"I got faith in you, babe," Vera said, smiling and pulling off.

Romell Tukes

CHAPTER 46
DARBY, PHILLY

Beth's stomach was now poking out, showing her pregnancy. She was on the back burner for a while. At least until her second baby was due. The only reason she got back into the midst of things was to protect Lil Jet. She knew he only hopped back into the field because he got shot.

Last week, she heard Twin got killed and that hit her and the gang hard, especially Lil Jet. Since Twin's murder, Lil Jet had been in and out the crib. He was not spending too much time with her or his own son.

Beth woke up to the doorbell. She was alone in her king size bed, wondering why Lil Jet ain't came home tonight, again.

She went to answer the door, knowing if it was Lil Jet, she was about to curse his ass out.

Beth opened the door with her wig twisted and crust in her eyes to see a gun pointed at her by a person she used to be cool with.

"You're just an innocent bystander," Lez told her.

"Nah, I'm Sosa Gang till the death of me," Beth said showing where her heart was at.

"I respect that. You was a solid bitch."

"I know and you're a traitor," she spat back.

"Can you blame me? Niggas came at me sideways." Lez used in his defense, thinking back to the night he had got shot by Sosa while talking with Foxy.

"Sometimes shit be a misunderstanding. A big one." She looked into the barrel of his gun that he still had aimed at her.

"If that's what you want to believe, then I respect it."

"Let's wrap this shit up. I'm tired," she says, ready to die.

"Okay,"

Boc, Boc, Boc, Boc, Boc ...

Lez saw Beth's body stumble into the doorway before falling and taking her last breath.

Lez had the drop on Lil Jet for two days now, but he was sick of waiting outside for him so today the message would get sent. He got in his SUV and drove off, listening to an old Jay-Z album. It was a song called Reasonable Doubt. The song Twin put him onto years ago when they was in Smith High school.

Hearing about Twin death hit Lez a little cause his beef wasn't really with Twin. His beef was with Sosa, but he knew if you fucked with one, you fuck with all.

Driving down the street, he passed a BMW with tints, but he paid no mind to the car thinking about Sosa.

***

Lil Jet pushed the BMW on his way home to take a shower and check on Beth. He hadn't been home in days because he was out hunting with the gang for Twin's killer.

Twin's death sparked a riot of angry shooters in the city, but nobody had a clue who did it, not even Sosa, so it was hard to have a starting point. Lil Jet believed it was Dirty or Rizzy and so did Lil Hak.

He pulled into the driveway and saw his front door open. Beth would never leave the door cracked. She used to be on his line about that. Lil Jet walked up towards his front door to see Beth's feet dangling near the door entrance. He rushed inside to see Beth laid out on the floor dead with bullet holes in her upper chest.

Forgetting about his son, he ran upstairs to see baby boy was still up there and alive. Inside the room, his son was sleep peaceful when Lil Jet took him out the baby carriage trying to leave. He couldn't walk past Beth's body again as tears rolled down his face. He left out the side door with the baby in his arms.

***

DOWNTOWN PHILLY

Sosa parked in the airport parking lot so he can catch his flight to Colombia to pay his mom a visit. The last time he saw her when she killed Bless and drank her wine next to his body.

Leaving Philly right now would be his best bet anyway because Twin's death had his gang going crazy in the city. Sosa Gang had been spinning all through North Philly and Northeast looking for niggas in Dirty crew.

For the past week, there had been sixty-two murders in Philly, stemming from Twin's death.

Yesterday, Sosa heard Beth got killed and he felt for Lil Jet because he knew how much his boy loved Beth. Plus, she was an official chick.

Sosa walked to the private jet that awaited him at 7 AM always almost every time he went out to Colombia. Elina'd been calling him since last night, but he wasn't really in the mood to chill or talk about how bad the feds wanted to arrest him.

Getting on to the private jet, he saw three guards all looking at him oddly. Normally, his mom would send one or two, at the most. He took a seat as he realized the pilot cabin door was wide open with nobody inside. Sosa felt a strange energy as he kept catching the guard peep at him. There was something completely off about everything today and Sosa wasn't gonna chance it.

In a quick motion, he pulled out his weapon and fired.

Bloc...Bloc...Bloc...Bloc...Bloc...Bloc...

Sosa killed two of them and hit the last man in his shoulder, running down on him.

"You speak English?" Asked Sosa with the gun to his large head. "Who sent you?"

"Your mom," the man spoke with bad English, but it was clear as day.

"Sent you to kill me?" Sosa wanted to make sure what he was hearing.

"Si, papi. She gonna kill you and take over Philly she says."

That was all Sosa needed to hear before he put two bullets and the man's head, instantly killing him. Sosa couldn't believe his own mom had been plotting to snake him this whole time.

Walking out of the jet, his mind was spinning crazy, thinking about how bad this situation could turn out.

The pilot was eating a bagel and drinking a cup of coffee, walking to the jet ready for takeoff.

"I was supposed to be on that flight bro, but this is what I want you to do. Take the flight to Colombia anyway and tell the woman I said nice try. I'll see her soon." Sosa handed him twenty thousand dollars.

"Yes sir, anything else?" The old white man asked.

"Yeah, don't touch nothing on the jet," Sosa says before walking off.

"Will do, sir. Thank you."

***

Bogotá Colombia

Ashley saw the private jet landing and a smile appeared over her beautiful face.

The plot to kill Sosa had been in her plans since she was in the nut house in Atlanta getting her thoughts together. She wanted Sosa to build a big foundation in Philly so she could come and take over. Sending the guards to take him out on his flight was perfect timing and easy so she wouldn't have to lift a finger.

The jet parked and nobody got off except an old white man stepping off the stairs looking around. She was looking for her guards to deliver the good news.

Ashley got out with her men to see what the fuck was going on. Something didn't feel right.

"You're the lady?" The white man asked Ashley.

"I guess but where the hell is everybody?"

"A young man in Philly told me to tell you nice try and he will see you soon or something of that nature," he told Ashley as she rushed up the stairs of the jet to see if her worst fear happened. Ashley saw all three of the goons she sent dead in the jet, slumped in pools of dark blood.

Sosa knew what took place and how she just tried to backdoor him. Now shit was about to go up. Walking out of the jet, she walked right up to the pilot and shot him in the face for no reason except for he was standing at the wrong place, wrong time.

CHAPTER 47
CHESTER, PHILLY
ONE MONTH LATER

Rizzy had been running around with his head cut off for the last month getting his bag up. His love life with Foxy had been going well. He just bought her an engagement ring about to propose to Foxy. The ring cost seven hundred thousand dollars but luckily, he got it for three hundred, which was his Rolls Royce money for one he planned to get.

He really wanted to spend the rest of his life with Foxy. She had every trait he loved and looked for in a woman.

Rizzy entered his apartment to take a nap to hear a TV on and the only person who had his keys was Foxy.

"Hey babe," Foxy said from inside the living room waving at him.

"What you doing here?' Rizzy asked, thinking if he should pop the big question to her now.

"I just figured I could come spend some time with you. It's been a week." She had not saw him in seven days and every time she called, he was too busy or driving.

"Oh, that's fine. I see you rocking my T-shirt." Rizzy gave her a wet kiss before walking into the kitchen acting like he was getting a drink but was looking for the ring.

"I got a surprise for you," Foxy yelled from in the living room.

"Okay, that's funny because I have one for you too babe." Rizzy finally got the box out and took a deep breath.

When he stepped into the living room, the box slipped out his hand hitting the floor as Foxy and Lez both aimed guns at him.

"You really a dumb nigga," Foxy says with a smirk.

"I should've known better." Rizzy didn't see this coming because Foxy always said how much she hated Lez. Now, she had a gun out on him with Lez by her side.

"We all slip up bro," Lez says.

"I'ma miss you." Foxy lied.

"I can tell." Rizzy knew it was over for him, so he didn't waste time in begging or pleading for his life whatsoever.

"We need to go be at that meeting in an hour," says Foxy.

"Bet," Lez replied before they lit up the apartment.

Boc, Boc, Boc...

Boom, Boom, Boom, Boom...

Foxy picked up the box Rizzy had in his hand before they killed him.

"This nigga was about to propose," says Foxy looking at the big diamond in the box.

"That's a big rock."

"Hell yeah. I'ma keep it anyway," Foxy said as they walked out of the apartment together.

Two months ago, Foxy and Lez got back together and came up with a plan to get rid of Rizzy but first they had to holla at Imam Ahmad and Janasia.

Once given the green light, it was on and popping. They plotted carefully, watching Rizzy's every step.

FISHTOWN, PHILLY
TWO MONTHS LATER

Vera came out to get her pussy and eyebrows waxed and a massage at a local spa. She'd been under the radar lately, building a solid business partnership with Imam Ahmad. She recently started to supply him and his crew, which had been a big profit for her.

"I have an appointment. The name is Vera DeRosario," she told the young Korean lady at the front desk.

"Oh yes, I see."

"Which room?"

"Six. All the way into the back." The Korean woman's accent was so strong as if she was new to America.

"Thank you." Vera walked down the dim hall to smell candles and incense burning in the air.

Vera got to the comfortable room undressed and laid down on the message table ready for her hot oil treatment massage before her monthly wax.

The only nigga hitting her and eating her coochie was Imam Ahmad. She didn't have time for nobody else's attention.

She stuck her face into the neck rest as the door opened, which meant it was time for her body treatment. Vera felt manly hands on her shoulders but normally women would give the body massage. The man started to get a little too rough as she wasn't liking the force he was putting on her.

"You're a little too—" Vera popped up to see it was Sosa behind her with his gun out.

"You pretty just like your daughter was before I had to kill her."

"Fuck you."

"I really did love her," Sosa says, seeing exposed nipples on her breast that were perfect like melons.

"You're smarter than what I gave you Sosa but together as a team, we can take over Philly," she said trying to buy time to get to her gun.

"Not another one of those stories, baby girl but I can't lie. You one sexy ass bitch."

"Maybe you can get a piece of this if you act right." Vera blushed, feeling a little fluttered by a handsome man such as Sosa was into her.

"I'll pass on that beat up shit," Sosa said pointing at her beat up pussy lip hanging out her thongs.

"Don't judge a book by its cover," she told him.

"That's a fucked up looking cover."

"Put the gun down and we can talk some things out because we really need each other, Sosa."

"The Outlaws want you dead and I can get you them on a paper plate," she tells him.

"Oh, a paper plate huh?"

"Yep."

"At what cost?"

"My life. Spare me, handsome."

"How would I know if I can trust you?" He asked.

"Well, you're just have to trust me and chance it."

"I'm not good with chances or trust. Sorry."

Boc... Boc... Boc... Boc... Boc... Boc... Boc...

Sosa killed her, watching Vera's body fall onto the floor as he left the room, completing his mission.

Killing Vera had to be done because she was becoming a very big, big, big issue for him.

With Vera supplying the Outlaws now, they would be without a drug connect. He was hitting their pockets first as his boy, Twin used to always tell him.

In a few days, Twin's birthday would arrive, and Sosa knew that was going to be a fucked up day mentally for him and the gang because Twin left a big mark on them.

Walking out of the spa, he used the backdoor as he saw people running out of the front in panic mode because of the gunfire they heard.

Sosa was parked in the back and made a safe getaway home.

***

DOWNTOWN PHILLY

Imam Ahmad called a small meeting in a remote area near a river and a bridge.

"Glad y'all here." Imam Ahmad got out his truck to see Foxy and Lez both standing there.

"So basically, good news, bad news," spoke Lez.

"I guess so but Vera, our plug was killed at a spa. I think she was supplying us," Imam Ahmad said as a Maybach and a SUV was pulling up.

"Fuck. I hate them niggas." Foxy knew Sosa Gang had to fuck up there plans.

"What's the good news?" Lez asked, thinking Janasia was in the Maybach showing up in style.

"You're about to find out right now," Imam Ahmad said as the driver of the expensive car got out and opened the back door. Ashley stepped out wearing heels and a dress, looking like a snack with her hair and nails done up.

"Who the fuck is that?" Foxy asked with a stank attitude.

"Our new plug and member," Imam Ahmad said.

"I thought we had a vote people in?" Foxy asked.

"The rules change when it comes to big business, and did we vote in your little boyfriend?" He looked at Lez as Ashley approached them.

"Hey," Ashley spoke to them all.

"Welcome. We're glad to have you Ashley," Imam Ahmad stated.

"I can tell," she replied.

"We shocked to be accepting someone new so fast but we're glad to have you. I'ma tell you now, we have a lot of beef right now. You may not make it a day out here," says Foxy as Ashley chuckled.

"My son won't be a problem. Y'all just don't know how to kill a Jaguar," Ashley stated.

"Your son?" Lez repeated catching that part only before his mind went blank.

"Sosa is her son," Imam Ahmad said.

"Ain't no fucking way we doing business with the enemy's mother," Foxy said pissed and ready to kill Ashley but there were six goons waiting for any of them to bust a move on Ashley.

"It's already a done deal," Imam Ahmad said.

"I'm outta here. Fuck this," Foxy said walking off.

"Go get your girl. I'll be in touch and make sure she does nothing stupid that will cause the both of you lives," says Imam Ahmad.

"Whenever it's meant to be, its meant to be," Lez said before walking off to leave with Foxy.

"Looks like you have some cleaning up to do," Ashley joked.

"I'll handle it."

"I hope so," Ashley said watching the car with Foxy and Lez inside take off, speeding.

"When will you be ready for our first dealing?" asked Imam Ahmad.

"Two weeks."

"Perfect."

"I'll call you." Ashley walked off.

Imam Ahmad looked at her ass and knew she had to exercise. He thought about how Janasia didn't show up for the meeting. He called to get no answer.

Imam Ahmad got inside his SUV leaving and thinking about bigger and better plans that he had in store.

**

SOUTHWEST, PHILLY

Lil Hak and Lil Jet caught their girl Janasia leaving work and snatched her up out of her car. They brought Janasia to a building in the slums.

"Look at your dumb ass," Lil Jet said, staring at Janasia who was chained to a wall beaten up badly.

"Die slow bitch," Janasia said breathing heavily, feeling one more hit would take her out for good.

"I like her," Lil Hak said.

"Fuck that bitch." Lil Jet spat in her face.

"Now that your dead, who do you think is going to take your place?" Lil Hak asked.

"I don't know, or care. Can you fucks just kill me and get it over with?" She asked as the spit dripped into her eyes.

"Be patient, bitch," Lil Jet told her waiting on a text back from Sosa to see what he wanted them to do.

"The two of you don't have a clue what you got yourself into," she told them seriously.

"Shawty we knew what it was before we signed up for this shit." Lil Jet added seeing a text from Sosa hit his cell phone that read KH … and that was code for kill her.

Boc, boc, boc, Boc, Boc …

Boom, Boom, Boom …

Seeing it was a job well done, both men left her in the abandoned building and went out to a club. It was something they did on the regular nowadays.

Sosa told them he would meet them at the club in a few hours. He was on something important right now.

"The DEA gonna be on us," Lil Jet said.

"No there not," Lil Hak replied driving to his favorite club.

"Nigga, she the head of the DEA." Lil Jet snapped back because Lil Hak think he knows everything.

"In her briefcase, I placed photos of Janasia with Imam Ahmad. I had photos with her hugged up with Lez," says Lil Hak

"You was following her bro?" Lil Jet had no clue Lil Hak was on it like that but that could be the reason why he barely saw him at certain hours of the day.

"When they find out she a dirty agent, the heat will be off us, young bull." Lil Hak smiled.

"Facts."

"I got us, bull."

"Where is Sosa anyway?" Lil Jet wondered.

"Maybe in sum pussy."

"Nah, I doubt that bro. Sosa been on some Casper the ghost type shit for the last few weeks." Lil Jet added.

"He may be on one of his own little private missions." Lil Hak knew how Sosa liked to handle certain things on his own.

"Let's turn up and pop some bottles in this bitch," Lil Jet said as they made it to the club.

***

SOUTH PHILLY

Dirty smelled like a dog pound as he laid in a trap house smoking heavily like there was no tomorrow. Putting the crack pipe to his lips was a feeling he loved and wished it could have found him years ago instead of now.

The last ninety days Dirty had been with his cousin Regan smoking crack. The first month he smoked up all his drugs and now Dirty was down to his last ten dollars.

Regan had a dealer coming through in a few minutes to give them some of that new everybody's been talking about in South Philly.

"Dirty." Regan walked through the bed sheets used as a door to see Dirty high as a kite.

"Yeahhh," Dirty slurred.

"The guy is coming upstairs. How much money you had?" Regan asked about to put all of their money together.

Dirty dug in his Old Navy pockets because he sold his Balmain and designer jeans to local dealers.

Boom... Boom...

Regan caught two bullet to the back of his head as his body fell right on top of the trap house's dirty mattress.

When Dirty saw Sosa step over his cousin's body, he just closed his eyes already knowing what he came to do.

"Cowards close their eyes before they die, not killers," Sosa said before firing six shots into Dirty's frail body frame, seeing he'd lost over sixty pounds.

He been had the drop on Dirty but knew he was too stuck on crack to leave so he played it out cool.

Sosa heard his mom was in town, so he had her on his mind heavy ...

To Be Continued...
Sosa Gang 4
Coming Soon

Lock Down Publications and Ca$h Presents assisted
publishing packages.

BASIC PACKAGE $499
Editing
Cover Design
Formatting

UPGRADED PACKAGE $800
Typing
Editing
Cover Design
Formatting

ADVANCE PACKAGE $1,200
Typing
Editing
Cover Design
Formatting
Copyright registration
Proofreading
Upload book to Amazon

LDP SUPREME PACKAGE $1,500
Typing
Editing
Cover Design
Formatting
Copyright registration
Proofreading
Set up Amazon account
Upload book to Amazon
Advertise on LDP Amazon and Facebook page

***Other services available upon request. Additional charges may apply

Lock Down Publications
P.O. Box 944
Stockbridge, GA 30281-9998
Phone # 470 303-9761

Submission Guideline

Submit the first three chapters of your completed manuscript to ldpsubmissions@gmail.com, subject line: Your book's title. The manuscript must be in a .doc file and sent as an attachment. Document should be in Times New Roman, double spaced and in size 12 font. Also, provide your synopsis and full contact information. If sending multiple submissions, they must each be in a separate email.

Have a story but no way to send it electronically? You can still submit to LDP/Ca$h Presents. Send in the first three chapters, written or typed, of your completed manuscript to:

LDP: Submissions Dept
Po Box 944
Stockbridge, Ga 30281

DO NOT send original manuscript. Must be a duplicate.

Provide your synopsis and a cover letter containing your full contact information.

Thanks for considering LDP and Ca$h Presents.

NEW RELEASES

SALUTE MY SAVAGERY by FUMIYA PAYNE

SUPER GREMLIN by KING RIO

BLOOD AND GAMES by KING DREAM

SOSA GANG 3 by ROMELL TUKES

Coming Soon from Lock Down Publications/Ca$h Presents
BLOOD OF A BOSS **VI**
SHADOWS OF THE GAME II
TRAP BASTARD II
By **Askari**
LOYAL TO THE GAME **IV**
By **T.J. & Jelissa**
TRUE SAVAGE **VIII**
MIDNIGHT CARTEL IV
DOPE BOY MAGIC IV
CITY OF KINGZ III
NIGHTMARE ON SILENT AVE II
THE PLUG OF LIL MEXICO II
CLASSIC CITY II
By **Chris Green**
BLAST FOR ME **III**
A SAVAGE DOPEBOY III
CUTTHROAT MAFIA III
DUFFLE BAG CARTEL VII
HEARTLESS GOON VI
By **Ghost**
A HUSTLER'S DECEIT III
KILL ZONE II
BAE BELONGS TO ME III
TIL DEATH II
By **Aryanna**
KING OF THE TRAP III
By **T.J. Edwards**
GORILLAZ IN THE BAY V
3X KRAZY III

Romell Tukes

STRAIGHT BEAST MODE III

De'Kari

KINGPIN KILLAZ IV

STREET KINGS III

PAID IN BLOOD III

CARTEL KILLAZ IV

DOPE GODS III

Hood Rich

SINS OF A HUSTLA II

ASAD

YAYO V

Bred In The Game 2

S. Allen

THE STREETS WILL TALK II

By Yolanda Moore

SON OF A DOPE FIEND III

HEAVEN GOT A GHETTO III

SKI MASK MONEY III

By Renta

LOYALTY AIN'T PROMISED III

By Keith Williams

I'M NOTHING WITHOUT HIS LOVE II

SINS OF A THUG II

TO THE THUG I LOVED BEFORE II

IN A HUSTLER I TRUST II

By Monet Dragun

QUIET MONEY IV

EXTENDED CLIP III

THUG LIFE IV

By **Trai'Quan**

216

Sosa Gang 3

THE STREETS MADE ME IV

By **Larry D. Wright**

IF YOU CROSS ME ONCE III

ANGEL V

By **Anthony Fields**

THE STREETS WILL NEVER CLOSE IV

By **K'ajji**

HARD AND RUTHLESS III

KILLA KOUNTY IV

By **Khufu**

MONEY GAME III

By **Smoove Dolla**

JACK BOYS VS DOPE BOYS IV

A GANGSTA'S QUR'AN V

COKE GIRLZ II

COKE BOYS II

LIFE OF A SAVAGE V

CHI'RAQ GANGSTAS V

SOSA GANG IV

BRONX SAVAGES II

BODYMORE KINGPINS II

BLOOD OF A GOON II

By **Romell Tukes**

MURDA WAS THE CASE III

Elijah R. Freeman

AN UNFORESEEN LOVE IV

BABY, I'M WINTERTIME COLD III

By **Meesha**

QUEEN OF THE ZOO III

Romell Tukes

By **Black Migo**

CONFESSIONS OF A JACKBOY III

By **Nicholas Lock**

KING KILLA II

By **Vincent "Vitto" Holloway**

BETRAYAL OF A THUG III

By **Fre$h**

THE BIRTH OF A GANGSTER III

By **Delmont Player**

TREAL LOVE II

By **Le'Monica Jackson**

FOR THE LOVE OF BLOOD III

By **Jamel Mitchell**

RAN OFF ON DA PLUG II

By **Paper Boi Rari**

HOOD CONSIGLIERE III

By **Keese**

PRETTY GIRLS DO NASTY THINGS II

By **Nicole Goosby**

LOVE IN THE TRENCHES II

By **Corey Robinson**

IT'S JUST ME AND YOU II

By **Ah'Million**

FOREVER GANGSTA III

By **Adrian Dulan**

THE COCAINE PRINCESS IX

SUPER GREMLIN II

By **King Rio**

CRIME BOSS II

Playa Ray

LOYALTY IS EVERYTHING III
Molotti
HERE TODAY GONE TOMORROW II
By Fly Rock
REAL G'S MOVE IN SILENCE II
By Von Diesel
GRIMEY WAYS IV
By Ray Vinci
SALUTE MY SAVAGERY II
By Fumiya Payne
BLOOD AND GAMES II
By King Dream

Available Now

RESTRAINING ORDER **I & II**
By **CA$H & Coffee**
LOVE KNOWS NO BOUNDARIES **I II & III**
By **Coffee**
RAISED AS A GOON I, II, III & IV
BRED BY THE SLUMS I, II, III
BLAST FOR ME I & II
ROTTEN TO THE CORE I II III
A BRONX TALE I, II, III
DUFFLE BAG CARTEL I II III IV V VI
HEARTLESS GOON I II III IV V

Romell Tukes

A SAVAGE DOPEBOY I II
DRUG LORDS I II III
CUTTHROAT MAFIA I II
KING OF THE TRENCHES
By **Ghost**
LAY IT DOWN **I & II**
LAST OF A DYING BREED I II
BLOOD STAINS OF A SHOTTA I & II III
By **Jamaica**
LOYAL TO THE GAME I II III
LIFE OF SIN I, II III
By **TJ & Jelissa**
BLOODY COMMAS I & II
SKI MASK CARTEL I II & III
KING OF NEW YORK I II,III IV V
RISE TO POWER I II III
COKE KINGS I II III IV V
BORN HEARTLESS I II III IV
KING OF THE TRAP I II
By **T.J. Edwards**
IF LOVING HIM IS WRONG…I & II
LOVE ME EVEN WHEN IT HURTS I II III
By **Jelissa**
WHEN THE STREETS CLAP BACK I & II III
THE HEART OF A SAVAGE I II III IV
MONEY MAFIA I II
LOYAL TO THE SOIL I II III
By **Jibril Williams**
A DISTINGUISHED THUG STOLE MY HEART I II & III
LOVE SHOULDN'T HURT I II III IV

220

RENEGADE BOYS I II III IV
PAID IN KARMA I II III
SAVAGE STORMS I II III
AN UNFORESEEN LOVE I II III
BABY, I'M WINTERTIME COLD I II
By **Meesha**
A GANGSTER'S CODE I &, II III
A GANGSTER'S SYN I II III
THE SAVAGE LIFE I II III
CHAINED TO THE STREETS I II III
BLOOD ON THE MONEY I II III
A GANGSTA'S PAIN I II III
By J-Blunt
PUSH IT TO THE LIMIT
By **Bre' Hayes**
BLOOD OF A BOSS **I, II, III, IV, V**
SHADOWS OF THE GAME
TRAP BASTARD
By **Askari**
THE STREETS BLEED MURDER **I, II & III**
THE HEART OF A GANGSTA I II& III
By **Jerry Jackson**
CUM FOR ME I II III IV V VI VII VIII
An **LDP Erotica Collaboration**
BRIDE OF A HUSTLA **I II & II**
THE FETTI GIRLS **I, II& III**
CORRUPTED BY A GANGSTA I, II III, IV
BLINDED BY HIS LOVE
THE PRICE YOU PAY FOR LOVE I, II ,III
DOPE GIRL MAGIC I II III

Romell Tukes

By **Destiny Skai**
WHEN A GOOD GIRL GOES BAD
By **Adrienne**
THE COST OF LOYALTY I II III
By Kweli
A GANGSTER'S REVENGE **I II III & IV**
THE BOSS MAN'S DAUGHTERS I II III IV V
A SAVAGE LOVE **I & II**
BAE BELONGS TO ME I II
A HUSTLER'S DECEIT I, II, III
WHAT BAD BITCHES DO I, II, III
SOUL OF A MONSTER I II III
KILL ZONE
A DOPE BOY'S QUEEN I II III
TIL DEATH
By **Aryanna**
A KINGPIN'S AMBITON
A KINGPIN'S AMBITION **II**
I MURDER FOR THE DOUGH
By **Ambitious**
TRUE SAVAGE I II III IV V VI VII
DOPE BOY MAGIC I, II, III
MIDNIGHT CARTEL I II III
CITY OF KINGZ I II
NIGHTMARE ON SILENT AVE
THE PLUG OF LIL MEXICO II
CLASSIC CITY
By **Chris Green**
A DOPEBOY'S PRAYER
By **Eddie "Wolf" Lee**

Sosa Gang 3

THE KING CARTEL **I, II & III**
By **Frank Gresham**
THESE NIGGAS AIN'T LOYAL **I, II & III**
By **Nikki Tee**
GANGSTA SHYT **I II &III**
By **CATO**
THE ULTIMATE BETRAYAL
By **Phoenix**
BOSS'N UP **I , II & III**
By **Royal Nicole**
I LOVE YOU TO DEATH
By **Destiny J**
I RIDE FOR MY HITTA
I STILL RIDE FOR MY HITTA
By **Misty Holt**
LOVE & CHASIN' PAPER
By **Qay Crockett**
TO DIE IN VAIN
SINS OF A HUSTLA
By **ASAD**
BROOKLYN HUSTLAZ
By **Boogsy Morina**
BROOKLYN ON LOCK I & II
By **Sonovia**
GANGSTA CITY
By **Teddy Duke**
A DRUG KING AND HIS DIAMOND I & II III
A DOPEMAN'S RICHES
HER MAN, MINE'S TOO I, II
CASH MONEY HO'S

Romell Tukes

THE WIFEY I USED TO BE I II
PRETTY GIRLS DO NASTY THINGS
By Nicole Goosby
TRAPHOUSE KING **I II & III**
KINGPIN KILLAZ I II III
STREET KINGS I II
PAID IN BLOOD **I II**
CARTEL KILLAZ I II III
DOPE GODS I II
By **Hood Rich**
LIPSTICK KILLAH **I, II, III**
CRIME OF PASSION I II & III
FRIEND OR FOE I II III
By **Mimi**
STEADY MOBBN' **I, II, III**
THE STREETS STAINED MY SOUL I II III
By **Marcellus Allen**
WHO SHOT YA **I, II, III**
SON OF A DOPE FIEND I II
HEAVEN GOT A GHETTO I II
SKI MASK MONEY I II
Renta
GORILLAZ IN THE BAY **I II III IV**
TEARS OF A GANGSTA I II
3X KRAZY I II
STRAIGHT BEAST MODE I II
DE'KARI
TRIGGADALE I II III
MURDAROBER WAS THE CASE I II
Elijah R. Freeman

224

Sosa Gang 3

Romell Tukes

By S. Allen
TRAP GOD I II III
RICH $AVAGE I II III
MONEY IN THE GRAVE I II III
By Martell Troublesome Bolden
FOREVER GANGSTA I II
GLOCKS ON SATIN SHEETS I II
By Adrian Dulan
TOE TAGZ I II III IV
LEVELS TO THIS SHYT I II
IT'S JUST ME AND YOU
By Ah'Million
KINGPIN DREAMS I II III
RAN OFF ON DA PLUG
By Paper Boi Rari
CONFESSIONS OF A GANGSTA I II III IV
CONFESSIONS OF A JACKBOY I II
By Nicholas Lock
I'M NOTHING WITHOUT HIS LOVE
SINS OF A THUG
TO THE THUG I LOVED BEFORE
A GANGSTA SAVED XMAS
IN A HUSTLER I TRUST
By Monet Dragun
CAUGHT UP IN THE LIFE I II III
THE STREETS NEVER LET GO I II III
By Robert Baptiste
NEW TO THE GAME I II III
MONEY, MURDER & MEMORIES I II III
By **Malik D. Rice**

LIFE OF A SAVAGE I II III IV

A GANGSTA'S QUR'AN I II III IV

MURDA SEASON I II III

GANGLAND CARTEL I II III

CHI'RAQ GANGSTAS I II III IV

KILLERS ON ELM STREET I II III

JACK BOYZ N DA BRONX I II III

A DOPEBOY'S DREAM I II III

JACK BOYS VS DOPE BOYS I II III

COKE GIRLZ

COKE BOYS

SOSA GANG I II III

BRONX SAVAGES

BODYMORE KINGPINS

BLOOD OF A GOON

By Romell Tukes

LOYALTY AIN'T PROMISED I II

By Keith Williams

QUIET MONEY I II III

THUG LIFE I II III

EXTENDED CLIP I II

A GANGSTA'S PARADISE

By **Trai'Quan**

THE STREETS MADE ME I II III

By **Larry D. Wright**

THE ULTIMATE SACRIFICE I, II, III, IV, V, VI

KHADIFI

IF YOU CROSS ME ONCE I II

ANGEL I II III IV

IN THE BLINK OF AN EYE

Romell Tukes

By **Anthony Fields**
THE LIFE OF A HOOD STAR
By **Ca$h & Rashia Wilson**
THE STREETS WILL NEVER CLOSE I II III
By **K'ajji**
CREAM I II III
THE STREETS WILL TALK
By Yolanda Moore
NIGHTMARES OF A HUSTLA I II III
BLOOD AND GAMES
By King Dream
CONCRETE KILLA I II III
VICIOUS LOYALTY I II III
By Kingpen
HARD AND RUTHLESS I II
MOB TOWN 251
THE BILLIONAIRE BENTLEYS I II III
REAL G'S MOVE IN SILENCE
By Von Diesel
GHOST MOB
Stilloan Robinson
MOB TIES I II III IV V VI
SOUL OF A HUSTLER, HEART OF A KILLER I II
GORILLAZ IN THE TRENCHES I II III
By SayNoMore
BODYMORE MURDERLAND I II III
THE BIRTH OF A GANGSTER I II
By Delmont Player
FOR THE LOVE OF A BOSS
By C. D. Blue

Sosa Gang 3

MOBBED UP I II III IV

THE BRICK MAN I II III IV V

THE COCAINE PRINCESS I II III IV V VI VII VIII

SUPER GREMLIN

By King Rio

KILLA KOUNTY I II III IV

By Khufu

MONEY GAME I II

By Smoove Dolla

A GANGSTA'S KARMA I II III

By FLAME

KING OF THE TRENCHES I II III

by **GHOST & TRANAY ADAMS**

QUEEN OF THE ZOO I II

By **Black Migo**

GRIMEY WAYS I II III

By Ray Vinci

XMAS WITH AN ATL SHOOTER

By Ca$h & Destiny Skai

KING KILLA

By Vincent "Vitto" Holloway

BETRAYAL OF A THUG I II

By Fre$h

THE MURDER QUEENS I II III

By Michael Gallon

TREAL LOVE

By Le'Monica Jackson

FOR THE LOVE OF BLOOD I II

By Jamel Mitchell

HOOD CONSIGLIERE I II

Romell Tukes

By Keese
PROTÉGÉ OF A LEGEND I II III
LOVE IN THE TRENCHES
By Corey Robinson
BORN IN THE GRAVE I II III
By Self Made Tay
MOAN IN MY MOUTH
By XTASY
TORN BETWEEN A GANGSTER AND A GENTLEMAN
By J-BLUNT & Miss Kim
LOYALTY IS EVERYTHING I II
Molotti
HERE TODAY GONE TOMORROW
By Fly Rock
PILLOW PRINCESS
By S. Hawkins
NAÏVE TO THE STREETS
WOMEN LIE MEN LIE I II III
GIRLS FALL LIKE DOMINOS
STACK BEFORE YOU SPURLGE
FIFTY SHADES OF SNOW I II III
By A. Roy Milligan
SALUTE MY SAVAGERY
By Fumiya Payne

230

BOOKS BY LDP'S CEO, CA$H

TRUST IN NO MAN

TRUST IN NO MAN 2

TRUST IN NO MAN 3

BONDED BY BLOOD

SHORTY GOT A THUG

THUGS CRY

THUGS CRY 2

THUGS CRY 3

TRUST NO BITCH

TRUST NO BITCH 2

TRUST NO BITCH 3

TIL MY CASKET DROPS

RESTRAINING ORDER

RESTRAINING ORDER 2

IN LOVE WITH A CONVICT

LIFE OF A HOOD STAR

XMAS WITH AN ATL SHOOTER

Romell Tukes

www.ingramcontent.com/pod-product-compliance
Lightning Source LLC
Chambersburg PA
CBHW070447260626
47161CB00004B/1225